A TALE FROM FYNECOUNTRY

Eppie Goyea

authorHOUSE®

AuthorHouse™ UK Ltd.
500 Avebury Boulevard
Central Milton Keynes, MK9 2BE
www.authorhouse.co.uk
Phone: 08001974150

Fynecountry is a fictitious country, and so are the places mentioned. Names, characters and incidents are all imagined. Any semblance to people, living or dead, establishments or events is purely coincidental.

First published by AuthorHouse   5/13/2010

ISBN: 978-1-4490-5035-1 (sc)

Printed in the United States of America
Bloomington, Indiana

This book is printed on acid-free paper.

Dedicated to Mayowa

1. A Tale From Fynecountry

It was two o'clock in the morning when Biletu Bonsala heaved a sigh of relief and slumped into his three-seat sofa. The sigh was so loud it could have woken up the family next door. Or maybe it did, sending the man in the adjoining flat into bouts of hacking cough. These bouts of coughing often disturbed Biletu, who many a times had wondered whether it was smokers' cough or tuberculosis.

He and this guy's family had never spoken in the eighteen months they had lived side by side. While he was more or less a loner, preferring to keep himself to himself, his next-door neighbour (his wife called him Papa Cletus), enjoyed loud religious music; he preferred this even to his television or conversation with his wife or children. His sing-along sessions infuriated Biletu who had to prepare lecture notes, slides, exam questions, and ended his days by crashing out on his sofa.

Papa Cletus's singing sessions came in three parts. The first started at 5.30 in the morning when the theme was praising God for waking him up into a new day and to plead with Him to accompany him to and from work. This continued even in the bathroom, in the bedroom while he got ready in his police uniform, and ended - or was no longer heard - when he got into his car for work.

The second group of songs was after work with the theme of victory over all his enemies, seen and unseen, known and unknown. God was to send His unseen but powerful angels to destroy them all so he could live his life peacefully, and become prosperous. The end-of-day songs were for God's specific angels whom he called by name, to surround his house, his bed, his family, and grant them all peaceful sleep and wonderful dreams. These gradually faded until the much-awaited peace and quiet which his neighbours had also asked God for.

Biletu had often pondered over the reversal of role in this family. In Fynecountry women were usually known for this show of religiousness. They tried to impress neighbours with their knowledge of the latest religious choruses, and even felt guilty singing worldly tunes. However Papa Cletus's wife had no chance. Mama Cletus's gentle nature was no match to the husband's ostentatious and domineering character. He had taken over! Each night when peace and quiet finally returned to Biletu's day, his sofa bore the brunt. He squeezed his entire hulk into it, tossing and turning until he dozed off. This item of furniture had its own history.

After only three hours' sleep, at precisely 5a.m., Biletu's well-deserved sleep was brought to an abrupt end by the Islamic call to prayer. *'Allah-ah-ah-ah akbah'* the noise came repeatedly. It was from a mosque about a mile away, yet it sounded like it was from next door. In fact, in his confusion, he thought his arch enemy had crossed the carpet from being a pastor to being an Imam. Biletu's immediate utterance was unprintable. He knew then that he had leapt from the frying pan into the fire. He had leapt from the university accommodation he occupied with his wife and child to live in town alone, next door to Papa Cletus.

2. Early Years

Biletu Bonsala was the second son of Mr. and Mrs. Tuara Bonsala of one of the villages in Fynecountry. They were God-fearing Christians and educationists. Tuara's parents belonged to the elite of their community, when they moved to Lebon to work for the colonial masters. As a young man, the grandfather served as cook/steward to the governor and received many favours because of his honesty. One of such favours was that his children, Tuara included, played with master's children and were sometimes allowed to watch local programmes in the early days of black and white television in Fynecountry. He and his siblings often mimicked the seductive, sexy dances seen in the Indian films. This met with chastisement from the parents who warned against 'copying bad habits' and 'sins against God'. The children were taught about faith and works; to be God-fearing also meant being honest and hardworking. They must have a good reason not to go to Church. Some Sundays saw Tuara and his siblings four times in Church. They attended the early morning prayers, the regular service, Sunday school after lunch, and the evening service. During the Lenten season, they even went to prayers before going to school.

Biletu's father was the only one who carried on this tradition to his adult life and family, although he too had to stop when life became more hectic. The siblings were convinced they had attended Church enough times to last them their lifetime. As the brightest of the children, Biletu was close to his father and went to Church with him regularly until he left for boarding school. There he was exposed to the wider world and other forms of religion; worship of the elements and sources of supernatural powers. It was then he was able to put into perspective some of his secret childhood experiences. He remembered times when, unknown to his father, he saw sacrifices of live goats and chicken to appease the spirits of their ancestors. Sometimes his grandmother sent him with gifts of palm wine and kola nuts to the local native doctor and traditional healer for their help in protecting the family from a measles epidemic that claimed many young lives in the community. In fact he still bore on his left cheek the feint mark made by Kaiwe to ward off the evil spirits causing him *kuta*, the local name for convulsions.

When, as a teenager, he questioned his grandmother about all this, he was told they were only giving to Caesar what was Caesar's. Biletu tried in vain to understand how they figured out what belonged to Caesar and what belonged to God. He saw no wisdom in all this and decided to associate with neither Caesar nor any god so he would owe no one. Owe not, pay not. The tenet of doing unto others as one would like to be done unto suited him fine. One could not owe morality any kickbacks.

From then on these unanswered questions about his early life and religious practices had a negative effect on him. At university his Church attendances were perfunctory if at all he went. Socially he was amiable and gregarious; and very studious. As the founder of the Crabsters Club, he proved he could influence and lead his peer. He was one of the fortunate students to live in the hostel near the canal where they used to watch crabs dart in and out of their holes. Over time, Biletu formed the habit of catching them for his stew. Rice and crab stew soon became his favourite dish. This remained a secret for some time as he always stayed behind while others went to the various canteens on campus. After some time, his frequent visits to the canal 'to admire the crabs' aroused suspicion. He had nowhere to hide when he was caught red-handed by Jingo. The empty shells were right there by the sink; and he could not explain the whereabouts of the contents except point to the steaming pot on the cooker. When asked what it tasted like, he lied that in fact that was the first time he was cooking it; he just wanted to taste it after his research into one of the enzymes produced by crabs.

The next day news was all over the hostel that Biletu had been feeding on 'the poor crabs' and would soon die from their poison. Biletu of course knew there was no truth in this as he had been enjoying them, poison and all, for months before Jingo's great discovery. When the poison threat did not work, his friends tried quotes from the Bible to blackmail him. Did he not know it was cruelty to animals? He was going against the sixth Commandment; he was a glutton; how could he, from a Christian home be committing murder?

Once he confronted a group of them about the chunky bits in their plates. John Bull tried to defend their own cruelty to animals; their source of meat was the clean government-owned abattoir on the way to Ismei. "So it was slaughtered, eh? Those poor defenceless cows!" The next line of attack was to label him a stooge; how could he from a well-to-do background bring shame on his family by hunting around for lowly creatures living in holes in the ground when he could afford a whole cow?

Well aware of their malicious intents, Biletu kept one ahead. They did not know what they were missing, he boasted to Jo. One of the enzymes was an aphrodisiac! The Crabsters club was born, and crab stews were the order of the day. Students no longer waited for the crabs to show up; but dug deep underground for them. The impact was soon felt in the canteens around. The caterers, most of whom were wives of staff, cried foul. The Crabsters Club was banned. The founder could not be bothered; he left shortly after for England, in pursuit of 'the golden fleece'. He had won a post-graduate scholarship to study Chemistry at a well-known university in London.

****

Among his first disappointments in the UK was the fact that there was no Students' Christian Movement around. He had been advised that this was a good forum to meet other students from Fynecountry. All the help he could get in his search for the YMCA was the location of the Yellow Pages. He eventually located the building along a very busy road in central London.

His former classmate welcomed him into his room; a cubbyhole compared to his room back home. High Tech, as his nick name was, was also from a wealthy family by Fynecountry standard; he had a good size room in his father's house and a big backyard for relaxation. How could he adjust to this? Biletu was offered the only chair in the room while the host sat on the single bed. Other items of furniture included a small cupboard and a collapsible table. The other amenities were shared, such as the kitchen and television. High Tech could not but read the disappointment written all over his friend's face; so he quickly offered an explanation. He was 'managing' in this place in order to save some of his government allowance for a deposit on a mortgage.

The visitor almost fell off the chair. How could a government scholar from a country such as Fynecountry, sent here to study and return home to develop his country, think of buying a house? The answer was clear; he did not intend going back to serve his bond. Biletu's sermon on patriotism and duty to his old parents fell on deaf ears. He was reminded of his comfort back home and how his father had invested so much in his education so he could in turn help the younger ones.

"By the way," said Biletu, "Why did you disappear suddenly without telling anyone? University was to start in September; but when I asked your brother, he said you left home in March."

"Don't remind me of my ordeal in the hands of the police back home. I went to report the theft of my new stereo equipment by a boy living nearby, and I ended up as the accused, making false claims against an innocent citizen. My father had to pay two thousand mintos to get me out. The boy was later seen showing off the stolen goods. When confronted, his gang threatened to inflict so much damage to my face I would not see my way back home, let alone to the airport to leave the country. Would you wait to see such threats carried out? Well I chose not to."

After devouring some home food, they went through some photographs of the houses he had gone to see, his likes and dislikes of each. Despite his friend's enthusiasm and optimism, Biletu was not impressed. His plan was to realise his dreams and return to serve his country. His next stop was the library where fate directed him to meet his future wife, Bintu.

Bintu attended the Government High School for girls in Ismei, a few miles from Lebon. She too was lucky enough to get a scholarship to study Maths Education in London, and was staying at one of the university's hostels not too far from the library. She was born Bintu Ahmed, daughter of the Chief Imam of a mosque in Ismei. Attendance at morning assembly in her government-owned school was mandatory. It was therefore no surprise that she was comfortable with the way of life in her new environment abroad. She started wearing the hijab only a couple of years before she left home and after a protest by a group of Moslem students in her school who felt they should be free to practise their own religion as well.

As the head girl, she was asked one morning to lead the assembly in prayers. "Dear Lord God...," she started. The nudge she received from Abib to remind her of her religious allegiance ached for weeks. "Oh, sorry. Em...em... *Bissimilahi...*," she started, stopping after a short piece of the Koran before she embarrassed herself. News of this soon reached her father who gave her a good talking-to and reminded her of the promise of the Koran to disloyal followers. From then on she was to dress as a true Moslem and move only in the company of fellow Moslems. So when she arrived in London, she was viewed with curiosity, since there weren't many around dressed like that in those days. Once she asked a West Indian friend where she could find a mosque, she didn't know what she was talking about. Others wondered how she could be anything other than a Christian when she was always singing along to the Sunday Songs of Praise on the common room television. The truth was, she was middle-of- the-road.

At first Biletu did not know how to handle the religious differences. But thankfully he did not have to work hard. She spent so much of her free time watching Top of the Pops or the soaps that her prayer times became irregular until they fizzled out completely. She even started answering to Beatrice, a name preferred by her white colleagues. She sometimes attended the nearby Methodist Church just to see Biletu; and her skirt and sleeves got shorter and shorter.

The young lovers did not quite know how to broach their intensions to their families; Bintu's task being the more difficult. She would have to explain why, of all the young Moslem boys who had sought her hand in marriage, she had chosen a Christian boy.

Their relationship initially met with objection from Bintu's father. However he relented because his youngest wife was a Christian-turned-Moslem. Bintu's mother died five years before she left for the UK. Win some, lose some, he concluded.

It was great relief for them when both families agreed to the union. Bintu mused at the fact that she would have to change her initials and her signature; BB. She practised it over and over. Which one would she write in the marriage register, the old name or the new? She wondered.

The early years of their marriage were blissful, with Junior arriving eighteen months later. The husband obtained a Masters degree in Chemistry while the wife obtained first degree in Maths Education.

They both returned to their native land successful citizens, to take up jobs in one of the newly-established regional universities; he as a lecturer in his field and she as a teacher in the staff school used by student teachers. Immediately word went around about the new arrivals; Bintu had become a trendy lady, the most fashionable in the establishment. They were happy to be back home, although some changes in the social life surprised them. Nevertheless they adjusted.

****

One evening they decided to go for a stroll to the staff club some distance from their flat within the campus. Sitting in a corner was a former classmate of Bintu's. She couldn't reconcile Bintu Ahmed with the woman just introduced as Mrs Beatrice Bonsala, wife of the new Chemistry lecturer. After a moment's hesitation and a good look, she said, "Are you not Bintu Ahmed, a former head girl at the Ismei Government School?" As if that wasn't enough, she added, "Oh, are you now Beatrice? Is that your born-again name?" She went on to recount, to every one's hearing, the incident at the school assembly years back. Turning back to Bintu, she asked, "Remember?" as if Bintu would ever forget that embarrassing moment. As far as she was concerned, either name would do.

During Junior's second birthday party which followed soon after that, an aunt prayed that Allah would spare their lives so they would all gather again to welcome another addition to the family. The shout of Amen and *Inshallah* was deafening. As far as Biletu was concerned, there was no such luck. He never wanted a large family.

The name Junior was arrived at after a long debate on who to name him after; Bintu's grandmother who none of them knew but who he was supposed to look like or Biletu's paternal grandfather who died exactly ten years to the day he was born. Both parents agreed to Junior as the most neutral.

Life was as normal as it could be. Bintu's step mothers rarely visited; which was acceptable to the young couple. Biletu's mother was too busy with the foster home and orphanage she managed. She felt lonely after own children flew the nest; and having been involved in Church charity work most of her life she decided to look after the unlucky little ones.

3. Crazymoney In Family Life

Biletu's application for sponsorship for a doctorate degree was successful and he had to leave his wife and child to go abroad again. Being lonely, and with much time on her hands, Bintu got involved in the social and religious life around her. Like many of her friends, she looked for ways to augment her salary. This seemed to be the vogue among men and women in the university circle. Alfred, an old friend, came to Bintu's aid. Pastor Alfred, as he was known, was in charge of the government-subsidised mass transit buses in the Ministry of Works. His job was to keep the Scania buses roadworthy and available to workers, and he single-handedly managed the budget allocated for staff and materials. Hence it was easy for him to spread his allocation to include whoever he chose. Bintu was among the chosen few, and was given contracts to supply spare parts about which she knew nothing. Rumours had it that Alfred did this in return for 'favours' from Bintu.

On one occasion she was to deliver spare parts to put one of the Scania buses back on the road after two months' hibernation in the work shed. Even though Andy the staff mechanic had submitted the list and catalogue prices of all the items needed, everything had to be suspended until Bintu returned from sick leave. It took a letter of complaint from the workers' union to force Pastor Alfred to find immediate solution. That was how Isiaka, Bintu's middle man, came into the picture. He purchased the items from the Bisibi market at discount prices which he never passed on to the university. Such chain of buyers was common in Fynecountry and was seen as a way of making the money go round. In this case, Isiaka's cut + Bintu's cut + Andy's cut = Pastor Alfred's cut = a cut from the departmental budget = a slice of the national cake.

Did someone say foul? That person did not understand normal life in Fynecountry where moneycracy thrived in democracy. It was a matter of the money of the people, from the people, to be distributed by the people, to the people above the people. Through moneycracy Bintu was able to augment her salary while the husband was away.

Crazymoney was the currency in many circles in this country. In most cases it soon disappeared from local banks into foreign accounts. During its short stay it swelled the capital through the high interest rates created by the banking lords for themselves. It sure made its presence felt during its circulation among the same concentric circles, through the ripple effect. Those outside the circles could only watch with envy while the lucky ones among them gathered the crumbs Every citizen proclaimed crazymoney an enemy, a curse to be avoided; yet everyone secretly or openly admired and pursued it. Its possession endowed the owner with the feel-good factor. One belonged; one had arrived. Crazymoney built around the owner a cocoon that insulated and blinded him from the poverty and destitution around him. Bintu wished very much to be reckoned with; and this she could not achieve, even with her husband's salary combined. Hence she had to find other ways.

****

She also became an active member of the Christian Fellowship Circle in her Church. Members hosted the meetings in turns, and these often went on late into the night. She was entrenched in this way of life when the husband returned home, having obtained his doctorate degree. He could not believe the many changes in his beloved country. Christianity had become so commercialised, it was almost beyond recognition. While many claimed to be Christians, they worshipped money, large and numerous properties, and lavish parties. The acquisition of fanciful titles was a closer and more authentic god than that of the true Bible owned and read by all Christians every Sunday, Wednesday, and Friday at services, fellowships and other gatherings that went by various names. There was no shortage of such meeting venues in this wonder-country, as almost any space was a potential prayer meeting place; be it a house, school hall, parlour, kiosk, shed. It would do. Nor did it have to be a large gathering; two people would do, as long as they could sing aloud, clap aloud, others would soon join. Presto! A new Church was born. It was given a name, and the formal opening ceremony was organised. The more the dignitaries that attended, the more the money collected.

Biletu refused to join any of these Churches. Rather than be one of the Joneses, he chose to be a Smith; a Smith who did not believe in the commercial show-biz of religiousness in his country in the name of Christianity. He, on the other hand, chose not to be religious to be civil, loving, honest and patriotic. He believed one could just be good.

The changes in Bintu also were unbelievable. She always had one meeting or another to attend. Church service was all day. If the husband could not look after Junior the little one went as well. Over time, these activities took priority over her domestic duties, creating rifts in their relationship. His observation of the disruption it brought to their family life did not go down well with Bintu, who saw him as the devil.

Her plan to host a fellowship meeting met with vehement objection from the husband. Most of the fellow Christians were from the university community, learned, and of good social standing. Why should she endure such humiliation? She had attended many such meetings hosted by other members. Maybe, praise worship and concentrated intercession right there in their home would melt her husband's rock-of-Gibraltar of a heart. How dared he stop her from holding the Fellowship in their flat? After all it was university staff accommodation, and she contributed to its upkeep. Did she not, for the sake of the family, augment her salary with proceeds from contracts she got from the Ministry of Works? Did she not give body and soul for this? Moreover, does the Gospel of St. Matthew not recommend getting rid of any part of the body that was in the way of serving God? So, au revoir to Biletu Bonsala. Her own version of Papa Cletus's songs was one she learnt in the Sunday school when she used to sneak there with a neighbour, unknown to her Moslem parents.

> *Get thee behind me Satan, get thee away*
> *I don't want anything to do with you today*
> *Get thee behind me Satan, get thee away*
> *I want to be a Christian soldier*
> *And learn how to pray*

Humming or singing this, she substituted Biletu for Satan. Get thee out of my life, Satan Biletu. The Fellowship was coming to her house to pray; and pray they would, with or without her satanic husband.

However, and unknown to Bintu, Caroline the Fellowship secretary knew better. She had arranged another venue for the meeting, to make peace. This humiliated Bintu and spurred her on in her decision to pack bag and baggage and leave her home.

Help was at hand from the maintenance department of the Ministry of Works. Action was to take place during office hours. Biletu was sure to be either on seat in his office, or on foot in one of the lecture rooms. He was one of the few lecturers one could count on to be doing what they were paid to do. Others were either chasing or executing contracts, or busy putting the proceeds away in the banks.

The day before 'operation get- rid- of- Satan', Bintu made a list of what not to take; that was easier and shorter. The three-seat sofa would stay behind to continue to give the much-needed succour to its regular user. It was not worth taking anyway, with the smell of Junior's vomit still lingering around it; a misfit for her new abode.

This was one of the few items left in the flat for Biletu. After a few weeks alone, he decided to move to a smaller place outside the campus. He thus became next-door neighbour to Papa Cletus.

****

Having become a loner, Biletu never frequented the university staff club like his colleagues did. What better place to enjoy the current news and campus gossips that accompanied the flow of pepper soup. The latest flings between lecturers and students for good grades, the embezzlement of chapel funds, the domestic violence in the Afiafa family, were flying like kites. Of course the show-down between him and his wife did not miss due attention.

Dr. Kwasa who lived in the flat below made sure he was present at the usually packed Wednesday joint, even though he was on crutches after a broken foot. He was in bed sleeping off his strong pain medication; so he learnt of it from his wife who was on school run at the time. But from the way Tim Kwasa related his account of the incident, one would think he witnessed it firsthand. According to him, a big lorry marked Ministry of Works came to do the job. Reading the expression on his colleagues' faces, he quickly added "Don't you know she has a boyfriend in the Ministry? Oh yes, he was the one who encouraged her to leave the husband; he has even furnished a new place for her."

He went on to tell how the husband happened to pop round unexpectedly only to burst into tears and then got down on his knees begging her not to leave him. While some laughed at the cowardice of the seemingly strong Dr. Biletu Bonsala, others expressed outright disbelief. The man they knew would do no such thing. "Oh yes," cut in Dr. Kwasa. "He was pleading like hell, actually crying." Tim Kwasa would have scored full marks, but for the appearance of Shehu, the post- graduate school representative who also came with another story of Dr. Bonsala. How the latter boldly challenged the Dean's decision on some examination results. When asked what day this happened, his answer baffled the keen listeners, because the Board was in session at exactly the same time as he was supposed to have been on his knees crying and trying to save his marriage. Glances went to and fro; Tim Kwasa quickly hobbled out.

4. Crazymoney In University Life

The Board meeting called to ratify the examination results for the semester was the most outrageous one Dr. Bonsala had ever been part of. As the current head of department, he had to present his students' grades which he had carefully prepared a week earlier and saved on his personal file. Previous experience taught him that such documents were eagerly sought after. Only he knew the hiding place.

The meeting scheduled for 11 o'clock finally started at 11:48.precisely. The argument sparked off by his exam results took him by surprise. The circulated list bore no semblance to his version which he gave Tarabo his secretary to type. Was he dreaming? Was he seeing right? Was he hearing right? He felt dizzy. How did J-J Atani get on the list for transfer to the medical school? He had the authentic list; where did the other one come from? He adjusted his bi-focal glasses and moved his gaze from one colleague to another. They all looked genuinely bewildered. Biletu was weird and non-conforming in his own way; but no one could fault his devotion to his work. He was one of the few no-nonsense lecturers who would not yield to kick-backs for grades. He wouldn't because he didn't need them. He would not be seen at any of the extravagant parties held regularly at various parts of Fynecountry; nor would he call one. He saved his salary a.k.a. 'pocket money' for rent of the small flat he moved into, fees for Junior's education, and some necessities for himself.

Tarabo's transfer to Biletu's department was neither accidental nor routine. He was posted there by design; with the hope that working with such a strict head of department would control, if not altogether block his corrupt activities. This man of diminutive stature was a well- known godfather within and outside the university. Although a grade two secretary by qualification, he had been given higher posts by officers too afraid to give him less. As the chief priest of the local egudu, a local god worshipped and revered by most in the land, he expected to get whatever he demanded in society. He was supposed to have cast spells on people, including Dr. Ibrahim who collapsed suddenly in the office and died. Story had it that he did not give Tarabo a free hand to order furniture items and reagents for the department. The deceased was too strict and insisted on scrutinising and having his signature on every document. Tarabo was not used to this; he must get rid of him. He did so with ease, rumours had it.

Many cases of examination fraud and mysterious results had been traced to Tarabo. For various sums of money he had altered grades for students; many of these went undetected. Some lecturers, even though suspicious, were too scared to confront him. Many tales of frustration were drowned in gossips and bowls of pepper soup at the staff club. Hence Biletu had no knowledge of 'the bench marker' – the euphemism given to this university secretary. Nor was he aware that Tarabo's posting to his department was like sending a naughty boy to detention camp. Naivety was written all over his face as he struggled to understand what was going on, and why his colleagues were taking things so calmly. Were they rejoicing at his distress and bewilderment? No. They knew the author of his dilemma; it was déjà vu.

J-J, a chemistry student, had approached Tarabo on the recommendation of former clients. As the first son of a business tycoon, he was under pressure to do well. He was to become a medical practitioner, and set up a private practice which would eventually grow into a big hospital to complement the existing successful Atani Enterprises. This ambition must be fulfilled at all cost; money was no problem. But money was exactly the problem that brought J-J face to face with Tarabo, and in the end sealed Tarabo's fate as a university employee. His luck ran out with Biletu Bonsala.

J.J. was going through life with the attitude that money could buy anything. He tried his best in secondary school and made good grades; they were just not good enough for a direct entry into medical school at Olito University. He therefore settled for the sciences, hoping for a transfer later. Like his father, he was outgoing and generous; he had both male and female friends. His lecturers were not left out of his gift lists; which in turn ensured good grades in his projects and exams. All of them except his chemistry don who he found a hard nut to crack. This one refused to succumb to the temptation of the brown envelopes or the father's social status. His father, the honourable chief, had already paved the way with the dean who was his friend anyway; and he got the assurance that all would be well. The dean trusted the chief's wisdom to prepare not just the arrival lounge but the whole of the tarmac leading to it. Unfortunately he did not take into account a customs officer whose cooperation was vital. This customs officer was not only his chemistry lecturer but also a member of the board that vetted transfers.

It was during their desperate search for a solution that J.J. was introduced to Tarabo.

Biletu, on the other hand, always put himself above board both when he found himself faced with hard decisions, and when he had been deliberately put in situations just to tempt him. Such was the case of Chief Professor Rev Joseph Indiko who thought that pulling rank with his titles would tempt Biletu to yield to the offer of the brown envelope. No luck. The (truly) honourable lecturer did not need the extra money being offered since he did not lead the showy life that necessitated money beyond his means. This happened only three weeks ago. This was why, when J.J. offered him a bribe to change his F grade to a P, he went livid.

."Please Sir, I'm pleading; and you will not regret it. I promise Sir, no one, absolutely no one will hear about this. And.... God bless you Sir ..... May He ..."

"Don't you give me that God anything! Get out of this office! Get out I say."

As he said this, Biletu made towards J-J Atani, his eyes like wildfire. The younger guy quickly made for the door.

Chief Atani was rich and influential. For him money could do everything. Despite his not-exactly- good looks and pot belly, he had managed to acquire two beautiful wives. Between them they had borne him five children. After four years of secondary education, he worked at the local post office for just over three years before he was able to save enough to register for the then-popular correspondence A-level course. Later on during his Marketing and Business studies he acquired extensive knowledge in trading and private business ventures. He soon created for himself a niche in Fynecountry's business activities. He belonged to several social clubs and religious circles. He knew people in high places in and beyond his native land. His benevolence touched all that knew him. He gave freely to family, friends and all the associations to which he belonged. Charitable organisations could count on him to donate generously to fund-raising events. In fact he gave so freely that there were rumours that some of his wealth was ill-gotten.

His family came first in all he did, sparing no expense in his children's education in private schools. The children grew up aware of their father's wealth and knowing he would go to any extent to get them through the best universities.

5. Moneycrazy Undercover

A new political scene in Fynecountry brought with it many changes at both national and local levels. New leaders, governors, directors, heads of departments and so on were appointed, while many lost their positions of power.

Among the latter was Alfred. The new Director of Works replaced him with his own man. Alfred would rather resign than work under someone junior to him. This brought changes in the equation; the pluses became minuses, with Bintu one of the latter. Contracts were no longer coming and the extra cash disappeared along with the supplier. Investigation into Alfred's time in office revealed the occupier of one of the properties being paid for by the Ministry. A quit notice was given to Bintu; and a few weeks to the deadline only the bedroom furniture and a fridge were left in her flat.

****

Biletu returned to his office one afternoon to find a brown envelope on his desk. He had become wary of brown envelopes and so was in no hurry to open this. His fears were allayed when he noticed the postage stamp. The ominous ones were usually delivered by hand. His eyes went straight to the signature of the sender. Was Chief Atani now seeking revenge? Had the broom of changes sweeping across the country reached his office door? Powerful individuals could easily influence such changes to hit back at their enemies.

The contents of the one-page letter were beyond belief. This man, he thought, must have added delusion of grandeur to his love of money, power and fancy titles. According to the letter, the chief's application to establish a private College of Sciences had been granted. He had thought long and hard for a forthright, hard-working and experienced person to be the provost. Could Dr. Bonsala name a date and time for further discussion? There were names for the other posts; but as he would understand, his was the most important, and needed to be settled first and foremost. Below the signature was the name in bold letters.

Biletu decided to give it a chance; under no circumstances though was he going to meet him in private. He was not taking risks. He wrote back, congratulating the chief on this worthy achievement. He felt honoured by this offer. Could they meet two days later at 11.30 a.m. in the university chemistry laboratory? His desk, although not within earshot of students, was in full view. He signed the letter, with his name in bold letters below, and enclosed it in a brown envelope.

On the appointed date and time, the honourable chief turned up in a grey suit instead of his usual flamboyant regalia; a deliberate plan to make himself less conspicuous. He had with him various documents such as letters of approval, site plans, budget projection etc. to support his dream of a college that would not only complement the effort of the university, but also give more young people the opportunity to fulfil their dreams while providing jobs for the local community. The meeting lasted one and a half hours at the end of which Biletu promised to consider the proposal, in light of what he had seen and the other names mentioned. They parted after a handshake. Subsequent meetings included others who had agreed to join the staff of the new college.

A lavish party was organised to welcome all staff and their families. It was to take place at one of the chief's several hotels. An invitation letter was addressed to Dr. and Mrs. Biletu Bonsala. It was a long time since he received a letter addressed to both of them, and he didn't know how to handle it. He was seldom invited to events anyway and only a few people (at least outside the university) knew they lived separate lives. In fact they never spoke until recently when he received news of Junior's hospitalisation following several episodes of convulsions. The local word for convulsion, when translated, implied something much worse than fits, and bore a stigma among the population. Bintu felt obliged to get from the husband more information about his own childhood convulsions. This was crucial in the diagnosis of febrile convulsion as against something more serious. He later visited the boy a few times at home in Bintu's flat after discharge. During his last visit he took the invitation letter with him, and supposedly forgot to take it from the window sill. On reading it, Bintu made a note of the date, place and time.

On the appointed day, Bintu got ready and with Junior stationed herself at a strategic location near the last turning into the road leading to the venue. She had instructed the boy what to do at the sight of his father's car; she had him practise a few times until she was sure it would work.

Biletu gave himself plenty of time to travel the five miles in his old jalopy. He was a careful driver, although gossip had it that he drove slowly because the old banger just could not move any faster.

As he turned into Hotel Road (as it was called), he had to slam on his brakes as a young lad ran out onto the road shouting "Daddy, daddy." He could not believe his eyes. Bintu's plan had worked. She opened the back door for Junior to climb in while she jumped into the passenger seat.

"Hello," she said; and that was it. He had no choice but to drive on to the venue where the honourable Chief Joseph Atani and a few others, including J-J, were standing with glasses of various drinks in their hands. The Bonsala family joined in; no one but those close to them would have suspected that the two were like strangers until a few minutes earlier.

When everyone had arrived, J-J who apparently was the master of ceremony, called upon Reverend Canon Dr. Dafid to open the gathering with a prayer. The Rev gentleman declared that he was praying in the name of the Father, and of the Son, and of the Holy Ghost. He invited the maker of heaven and earth to descend into their midst; bless the gathering and what they were about to eat and drink. Would the merciful Lord please help them in the worthy cause they were about to embark on and make them honest labourers in His vineyard. May the new College yield good citizens for His glory. Amen. The Chief lived up to expectation, sparing no expense in making sure they all had a good time. He in turn enjoyed all the compliments.

Dr. Biletu Bonsala, now the Provost, was called upon to say the closing prayer. He almost had a *kuta*. It was a long time since he prayed in private, let alone in public. After a moment's pause he took the plunge. "God of Abraham, God of Isaac, God of Jacob," (He secretly hoped he had them in the right order). "You move in mysterious ways to perform your wonders. What an amazing grace! Oh for a thousand tongues to sing your praises! Help us to march onward like Christian soldiers (he meant no offence to non-Christians) and build an exemplary establishment to your glory. Keep Satan behind us so we have nothing to do with him." At this point he had an eye open to watch Bintu's reaction. "Help us to gather in only the wheat, and weed the chaff. May we resist temptations no matter how great." He restrained himself from adding 'even temptations of brown envelopes'. "...Unite us in your love so we can all live and work together as one family. Amen."

There followed a lot of pleasantries and handshaking.

The outing was an unusual one for Biletu to say the least. He could not remember the last time he was out of his house so late; nor did he look forward to the drive back home, especially as he had to make a detour to drop his passengers. He was thinking of a solution when he heard himself say aloud "But I have no bed, only a sofa."

To his astonishment Bintu replied, "And I have no sofa, only a bed." Their eyes met and both burst out laughing. He felt both shame and nervousness as he drove towards the location of the bed, which was the closer and more sensible option in these circumstances. The Bonsalas were back together.

Since Biletu accepted the offer of the new job, he noticed that, for reasons he himself could not explain, Papa Cletus's antics were less annoying to him. Was it because their days together were numbered? Or was it because of a hidden agenda? He was not sure. He broke the ice by offering him shelter one day when he was locked out in the rain, and prevented him from battering his wife on her return. By the time Biletu moved out to start a new life with his wife and son, he and his neighbour were in good terms. It was no surprise that the job of security officer in the college went to Papa Cletus. Better a Satan you know.

A few months into her husband's new job, Bintu dared to voice something she had thought about for some time. She would like to start a private nursery school, to ease the pressure on the university staff school where she worked.

"No," replied the husband; "You can transfer your experience in supplying motor spare parts when the maintenance department takes off."

She left with her head bowed. Watching her like this was very gratifying to a man who once was left with only a sofa to rest his back, but who now controlled a whole academic establishment.

6. Blissful Ignorance

The College of Sciences under Dr. Biletu Bonsala took off on very good note. The contract for each member of staff stated clearly not only the job description, but also the code of conduct with regards to college affairs. Reaction to this was mixed. Applicants included some of his colleagues in the university; but he was too wise for that. He knew the ban on the daily two-hour absence supposedly for school run would not go down well with them. He wasn't even going to try and beat them; he would just avoid them.

No attempt to teach old boys and girls new tricks. Catch them young and keep them on track was one of his maxims. Nevertheless the young ones still got together to negotiate unions, but these never survived beyond a few meetings. He earned himself the nickname of 'The Headmaster' because of the spot checks he conducted on staff. He once noticed a physics class without a lecturer. This resulted in a query. On the internal telephone he went tap, tap, "Dr. Meredith, can I see you in my office please in the next five minutes?" "I'll be right over Sir, as soon as I finish in the lab." Although not in the lab where he should be, at least he was in his office to take the call. Wilson Koleson was not so lucky. He got a query for being absent from the college grounds when he was supposed to be in a lecture hall.

The college standard was the envy of neighbouring countries, and students came from far and near, with some going on to medical school in Lebon.

The first taste of trouble for Provost Bonsala came when the heads of departments sought for autonomy and less scrutiny in the day to day running of their schedules. Among their demands were departmental cars and drivers, automatic admission for staff relations, and interest-free car loans.

Biletu made careful note of all their demands and promised to consider each one and communicate his decisions in due course. He chose to do this because among them was young Peter who he thought had a streak of rebellion in him and might prolong meetings unnecessarily. Before the end of the week all senior members of staff had brown envelopes delivered to their tables marked 'private and confidential'. They were from the provost.

The memo read:

Dear Colleagues,

May I start by saying how lucky I am to have such wonderful and hardworking staff in this young institution established for the good of our country. I congratulate you all for what we have achieved so far. As you all know, this is a private institution, and I'm only a caretaker. After a long and realistic deliberation with the Proprietor, the following conclusions were reached.

It is both unfair and time-consuming for the provost to do the job of headmaster – as you called it – as well. He will therefore delegate the enforcement of the day to day running of the departments to the heads. Henceforth it will be their responsibility to ensure self discipline within the department.

We all rejoiced at the August 4th publication in the national newspaper The Vendor, referring to our college as a centre of excellence and the best in this region of the continent. How then can we recommend that anything, I repeat anything, be automatic? Was your admission into university automatic? Remember, we all want our children to follow our example of hard work and take pride in their achievements.

Departmental cars are good in principle; but few freebies should be expected from this college right now. Moreover, with each car must come a driver. The college cannot afford that now. As a concession there will be interest-free loans to anyone wishing to buy cars, with repayment plans as agreed with the banks.

Official accommodation is not possible in the foreseeable future. It is a desirable venture; but issues such as land and funds are not easy to settle. But we will look into it. In the meantime I implore each and everyone to please press on with the building of the good name we have established.

Thank you.

At the end was his signature.

A few days later, it was the provost's turn to get a brown envelope inviting him to a meeting to discuss the contents of the memo. The attendance was one hundred per cent; many came with pieces of paper on which they had scribbled questions and points to raise. The provost came with his piece of paper. No; it was not just a piece of paper; it was in fact a copy of the memo which he had sent out earlier.

He welcomed everyone; then went on to read the memo out loud. At the end he added, "Good day, and God bless."

As he made a move to gather his papers and leave, Tamara, the only female staff so far, rose up and said with obvious anger; "Excuse me Sir, are we not allowed to react to this, this, this thing you've just read?"

"React! As if I can't recognise reaction when I see one! Wilson's lower jaw was about a foot from the upper one; Apollo's glances moved from one colleague to another; I could hear Tyndale's breathing from here; and you, Miss Tamara Popou, were half sitting half standing. What more reaction am I to expect?"

"I mean Sir, to allow us express our views on the contents of your memo to us."

Looking at his watch, "Well, I guess you have a spokesman. You can express your views through him; or her. I'm afraid I have a lecture now. I also teach you know, and I don't want to be late." He led the way out while the others followed.

Two days after this meeting, on a Friday afternoon, Biletu got into his car to go home, but the car did not budge. The coughing and vibration of the engine attracted the attention of everyone, staff and students included. News had it that a similar thing happened the previous day outside a supermarket. He had to do the shopping because Bintu had backache caused by carrying heavy shopping. He had to wait until his mechanic came to his rescue. It served him right!

Biletu noticed that his son had been unusually quiet and unhappy for some time. On his return from Sunday school that weekend, he was asked by his father for 'a chat'. It turned out that the lad had been a victim of bullying both at school and in Church. Reasons included the fact that his father was a bully, so the son had to have a taste of the bitter pills he was always dishing out. His father was a scrooge, a miser. The college was rich, but he would not let others enjoy. He was not normal; he should be in a monastery. He had caused ill health to his poor wife. Even his son was beginning to show signs of emotional problems.

"Why has Big Uncle," (as Junior had started calling Chief Atani) "not bought us a nice car like his own and given us nicer place to live in?" the boy asked.

The older man was overwhelmed and at a loss as to what reply to give his son. At the same time he secretly admired the wisdom of such young man. Deep down he felt ashamed and sorry. He apologised to his son and promised to find ways of making life easier for him. Later that evening, for the first time in ages, the family went out to a nearby restaurant for a meal. Most of those present were youngsters. That set him thinking of what to do for his family life. He had never given it much thought.

A few weeks after the car episode, an invitation came for him to attend a Provosts' conference in Lebuka. It was too far to drive so he would go by air, fare paid by the college. The journeys to and from the airports, the conference venue, and around town he would do by taxi; problem solved.

The plane was forty-five minutes late, which set his blood pressure rising. In Lebuka, he hailed down about eight taxis before one agreed to take him to the venue for an extra amount because the normal route was blocked due to an accident. The ride was an experience of a lifetime, as the taxi stopped every few minutes, looking for more passengers. Is this not a taxi? The driver finally moved on in earnest with two passengers beside him and three in the back seat. The provost knew better than to complain; he was already late. In any case, what he thought was strange must be the norm since his fellow passengers did not complain.

At the conference venue he watched as his colleagues (other Provosts) came and went in their official chauffer-driven cars marked clearly as the Provost, College of various institutions. He began to feel uncomfortable standing outside the conference hall, wondering how to get to his accommodation. He found himself lying when asked where his official car was that the driver had gone 'to do the tyres'. That did it. He Biletu, could not uphold his pride to a colleague! When the next colleague came along, he did not wait for questions, but quickly accepted the offer of a lift. From then on he found himself secretly admiring the comfort being enjoyed by others at no cost to them whatsoever. The various institutions bore the cost.

As he lay in his bed that night he reminisced over his life in general; his ideas and ideals, his goals, his attainment so far, his philosophy of life. His thoughts dwelt for some time on his family life. Had he been a good husband, a loving father? How best could he solve the difficulties Junior was going through, perhaps as a result of his style of leadership? But how could honesty and forthrightness be wrong? How could waste and misuse of scarce resources and embezzlement of public funds be normal and acceptable? How could leaders of private and public establishments not be more accountable to those they served? Or, could be the subjects were not asking for more because they didn't think they deserved better? These questions kept popping up without any answers in tow.

At the end of the conference he condescended to accept a lift to the airport. He had just enough in his pocket for the fare home. He worried that he might not be a welcome sight; but the hugs and kisses assured him he was still loved, at least by his family. As he lay down for the night, he could not help going over the events and experiences of the past few days: the physical struggle, the annoyance, embarrassment, and even the shame he endured. Did he deserve it? Was it the fault of the social conditions around him? Above all was it worth it? This last question he deliberately chose not to dwell on or answer. He managed to drift off to sleep.

****

He was going through his mail in the office the following day when there was a frantic knock on the door. Without waiting for an answer, Bintu barged in, waving a brown envelope. What on earth had come on her, and what could it be that could not wait until he got home? A few weeks before then he would have screamed at her; but Junior's plight touched his heart so much, even Bintu benefited from his resolve to be kinder at home. But work? Work was a different matter. Work should remain strict and official.

The content of the brown envelope, Bintu declared as she took the letter out, was her appointment as the headmistress of the University Staff School. The job came with an offer of house allowance or university accommodation, and an official car. It turned out that the latter was a two-year old Peugeot station wagon used by the former head Mr. K. Alati, and of course it came with an official driver. She had free use of the car and driver, expenses paid by the university. Like her predecessors she planned to enjoy her new post, including out-of-state visits to her father and mother-in-law. Wow! Bintu's husband didn't quite know what to think of this; but on the whole, he was glad for his wife. In fact, he helped her draft the letter of acceptance.

Over the next few weeks some strange feelings started to take hold of Biletu. Apart from his changed attitude towards his wife and son, he could not help feeling some jealousy of his wife's progress and new social status. Also the freedom! No. He did not wish her evil; in fact he secretly wished the same for himself. But he lacked the guts. He enjoyed the occasional rides in the station wagon, even when he had to be dropped at his office. At first he felt embarrassed, but his old banger left him with no choice.

A few days later an urgent message came from his mother; she thought she was dying and would like to see him. He did not know what to do. He loved his mother although he had not been in touch as often as he should have been; his car was spending more time at the mechanic's than at his service. He did not feel it was right to use Bintu's official car; so he decided to go by public transport.

7. Mixed Encounter

At the transport depot, he was bombarded by touts looking for passengers for their own make of 15-seater buses. Biletu, a novice at this type of bedlam, based his choice on the one he was told would leave first - in eight minutes. Two more passengers entered. Surely the bus would soon leave.

However he got a shock when he looked around him only to find that the bus was half empty. What happened? Where had all the passengers gone? "Are you new around here? Don't you know the tricks of these chaps? Those people are not passengers; they are all touts who go around filling buses to lure travellers into believing they are ready to move." The voice came from one obviously seasoned traveller sitting behind him. Angry, Biletu got up to leave. "Where are you going?" said the voice again. "You will only go and start all over again; they are all the same."

He stayed put; but could not understand the calmness and sense of resignation around him. "I guess they are used to it," he concluded. The bus finally moved fifty-five minutes later. Biletu suddenly remembered that the man who collected the fares did not give him change. When he asked the driver, the reply was "His name is at the back of your ticket; he'll be here again tomorrow if you want to get him." Not understanding the sarcasm, he actually searched the back of the ticket.

As the bus sped along the narrow roads, the novice knew there was no way he would return the same day. He would have to stay in the village overnight and brace himself for the journey back. His twin cousins were the first to see him, each declaring how glad they were to see him after a long time. Then came Habibah, who used to live next door but who told people she was blood relation because of their privileged background. Others soon joined to welcome him; the young ones struggling to get his bag into the house. The sight of these old faces aroused suspicion that something was amiss.

"Is Mother alright?" he asked with genuine concern.

"Of course," was the reply "Don't you remember tomorrow is the tenth anniversary of Father's death?"

"So what?"

"So there's a memorial service in Church on Sunday."

"Surely that's not the reason for the urgent message from Mother?" By this time Biletu was face to face with his mother who was so overjoyed to see her son, she broke into songs and dances. The figure before him was far from sick or dying.

"Welcome, welcome my son; glad to see you. How's Bintu? Is Junior well? How's work? How was the journey?" All came out in one breath, leaving Biletu at a loss as to which question to answer first. "Mother we are all well. But I was expecting to find you in bed or critically ill in hospital, according to the message that came to me."

"Me ill? Who sent you the message? And who is this wishing me to die? God forbid! I will not die until I see you in your Mercedes. Anyway, you are welcome. Go and change and have a bath. Your food will be ready soon."

"But Mother, I still don't get it; what am I here for? I can see you are well and far from dying. Why have you put me through the horrible experience of travelling here by public transport?"

"Well you see, your own Mercedes would have been a lot more comfortable. Never mind, it's good to see you." The voice was that of Charles, a former classmate. He went into business soon after leaving school and was now a trader in the village, selling, among other things, linoleum. He would later proudly show Biletu how he had transformed his mother's kitchen floor.

After a refreshing bath and sumptuous meal, the visitor decided to walk round his father's compound, greet the rest of the extended family, and reminisce a bit. As some of the orphans came out to see the stranger, Biletu secretly admired and envied the way of life; quiet, relaxed, clean, contented. No hassle, no suspicion of one another, no stress. How he loved to be back; not now, some day. Some day, after he had built his own house in the small plot allocated to him in his father's will; when he had earned enough pension to live comfortably for the rest of his life. But will his pension provide him with the comfort he desired, deserved? May be not; maybe he would need more; in which case he had better start now, providing for his retirement.

His thoughts were interrupted by his mother's voice calling him by his pet name 'Kalima' meaning 'my joy'. After calling, she went straight to sit in her favourite seat, an old arm chair, waving her big raffia fan which she used to ward off mosquitoes. She brushed off some imaginary dust from the folding chair beside her and signalled to him to sit down for a private chat.

Sensing trouble, he made up his mind to be as calm as possible; he would let her do most of the talking while he would just listen. She repeated how glad she was to see him. She had used the anniversary of his father's death to discuss with him some burning issues which she had kept to herself for some time. She expected some comments from him, but since none came, she continued. "How is Junior?"

"Fine."

"Hmmm… Is he going to be Junior forever? When will he be senior? I mean, senior to a junior one?" No reply.

"Kalima are you listening? You book people have forgotten the village language. I am asking you when Bintu is going to produce more children for you; more grandchildren for me." And after a pause, "Now you understand?"

"Hmm…..." This time it was from the son. Provost and mother were having a tête-à-tête.

"If she is having difficulty, let me know so we can do something about it. After all we too have alternative medicine just like the white man."

"What do you mean, what methods are you talking about?"

"You first answer my question. Is she having difficulty? Or maybe you are planning your family?"

"Yes mother; you know how things are these days. One has to plan."

"Your plan is too long. Don't you think it's better if they are close so they can grow up together, play together, go to school together …"

"Yes mother; and cry together, fight together and spend all my salary together…."

"Now that brings me to the next point that is bothering me; your salary. Everyone is complaining that salaries don't reach far these days; that's why many refer to it as pocket money. God has been good to me I don't depend on you for anything, although your brother and sister help occasionally. But I hear you are not living up to the standard expected of the provost of a college; a famous college that should be paying you twice what you are getting. Can't you see you are cheating yourself? You drive a car that breaks down every other day and even borrow your wife's car. God forbid. How did she get that car anyway? That woman is wise. You think you are wise? You are not. You'd better open your eyes wide. She has a brand new station wagon whilst you can't even boast of a second-hand car; you drive a third-hand one. Oh my God, oh my God….." Biletu thought she was joking until she saw floods of tears flowing down the old woman's cheeks.

"Mother what's all this? And who has been feeding you with all these lies? He got up to go to his room. "No don't go. I'm only concerned for you my son. You know I don't have the time to visit you and my lovely grandson; I only depend on stories I hear from people who travel and hear what others say about you."

"What do they say (not that I care)."

"They say you are very efficient in your work as a provost. But you are tooooo strict, and tooooo miserly with the budget; and you don't take care of yourself."

"But you said I looked well when I came in. How come you are now saying I don't look after myself?"

"I don't mean that. I mean....they say that you don't enjoy life by spending the money at your disposal. After all who will query you? You see what I mean? Even your wife is now ahead of you. Kalima you only live once and I want to see you live. I'm not asking you to steal, but take what is yours."

"I've heard you mother, thank you."

"About the Sunday service, it's...."

"I will not be here; I'm leaving tomorrow. I'm glad you're well. Thanks again for your advice. I'll think about it." He surprised himself about how much sincerity he put into the last statement.

The rest of the evening and the following morning saw people going in and out of the house; some to help with the preparations, others just to nose around or see the new comer about whom they had heard so much. Charles brought some home-made brew to entertain his friend and convince him to stay for the Church service. He was the coordinator and would be seen not to have done his work well, "Although," he added "it is really your shame if you do not attend your father's remembrance service." Biletu went on to recount his experiences the last time he attended Church and his disgust at the way preachers extorted money from the poor congregation.

"But this is for your late father. Can you imagine what people would say if, after seeing you here now you disappear before the service? Please don't embarrass the family. I know you've been away for a long time, but you are still part of us. Please stay."

Biletu agreed to stay on one condition only: that there was to be no collection of any sort. Charles agreed, daring not to mention money they had already paid up front in order to have the date and time allocated. He would personally take him to the bus depot in time for him to catch the last bus back.

The Church was the same they all attended and were very much part of when they were young; but it was now full of new faces and things were very different. There was a lot of dancing and celebration of a worthy life. Biletu could not believe the large turnout, most of whom did not know the deceased. On the one hand he felt left out by his brother and sister; on the other hand, they must have the extra cash to organize such lavish ceremony for a man who taught them honesty and modest living. To him, all this was just an unnecessary show of wealth.

Charles knew exactly when to get his friend out of the place to avoid any unpleasant scene.

"Time to leave now, before you miss your bus," he whispered into his ears. "You get your things from the house while I get my vehicle. Don't let anyone know you are leaving."

Ten minutes later, Charles was outside, revving his engine. "Ready?" revving the engine louder.

"Is this….? Is this….?"

"Oh yes. This is my new faithful. I sold the old one a few weeks ago to a business colleague. The back seat has been cleared to make space for you. Let's go."

"When you were talking of vehicle I thought you meant a car!"

"Well this is my two-wheel vehicle. That's all I need and I'm happy. Sit down, let's go".

"Thanks."

He again surprised himself by making the sign of the cross on himself before sitting close behind the driver. There was no point in further conversation, as any other noise was drowned by that of the motorcycle.

The don felt both belittled and humbled at the same time. He who was revered by learned colleagues found himself being ordered by a village trader. At the same time he admired the man's relaxed personality, friendliness and obvious contentment with his life in the village. Charles seemed to know everyone at the bus station; so his friend had no problem getting a front seat. A repeat of his former experience would not surprise him. But worse was awaiting him. For the first thirty minutes he enjoyed the journey; fresh breeze blowing in his face. At first it was gentle; but as the bus sped along it became rather uncomfortable. Then the drive through potholes and rugged parts of the road slowed down the journey considerably. What started as warmth on his backside soon became heat. It was a case of cool breeze on the face, deep heat below. He shuffled his bottom from side to side trying to make himself comfortable, but to no avail. When he could no longer bear it, he resorted to the lingo, thinking it would help.

"My backside is on fire!" he shouted.

"Cool it man. Cool it." replied the driver coolly.

The whole bus erupted in laughter.

"Why don't you remove your jacket and sit on it; maybe there's only a fine line between your bottom and the engine," added a passenger.

Another bout of laughter followed. Relief came only when a passenger left and he was able to take his place. Biletu bore the humiliation quietly.

Husband and wife were delighted to see each other. Bintu had been worried for his safety on the village roads. There had been incidents of armed robbery on the narrow roads. She asked if her mother-in-law liked the long casual dress she sent her. She liked it very much, he said; and she sent her thanks. She could not send any farm produce since he travelled by public transport; but she sent her daughter-in-law an old necklace of hers as a keepsake. At the end of the short note accompanying it she wrote 'from Mamabless'. Although her children called her Mother, she was known in the village as Mamabless because to every greeting, she replied "Bless you". This note was to be of immense help to Bintu later. Biletu knew better than to relate the other aspects of their conversation. Junior asked after his grandma and his playmates who he had met only once during his one and only visit to the village.

That night, back in familiar surroundings, Biletu again went through his experiences of the last few days; and indeed the past few years. There was introspection into his own personality, outlook, relationships with people around him, and the effect of all this on his life. He tried to piece together his family background, childhood teachings, some significant others who might have influenced his way of thinking. He even reminded himself of some theories he came across in his philosophy classes at university; theories of nature, nurture, of freedom of choice and responsibility in adult life, etc. etc. For several nights he slept little, tossing and turning in his bed till daybreak.

Even Junior saw the changes in his father. One day he remarked to his mother. "Daddy talks to us more now; he also comes home early from work." Bintu agreed with the young lad, but quietly wondered how long it would last. At least he was making an effort.

8. Bold Encounter

Things actually started to get better between them. Interaction between them became more constructive. Biletu went home with news of what was happening at work, sometimes even including his plans for the following day; what meetings were coming up, the agenda, and even what he intended to do and say. Junior's homework received daddy's touch every now and again. An unusual event was a day in the park. Those who saw them there could not believe their eyes. What was happening? Tongues began to wag; Bintu must have found herself some love potion; and it must be very powerful to be having any effect on her husband. Others said the gestures were in return for the use of the station wagon. That can't be, yet others proffered. There were definite changes in his relationship at work as well. 'The Headmaster' was becoming relaxed with his staff, delegating some powers to trusted colleagues who in turn began to respect and support him more. Further changes were prompted by an unusual incident.

It was the young rebel Koleson who one day approached him 'to speak his mind'. On the one hand he really and truly admired the provost for his dedication to work, his uprightness, and his sacrifice. Only a few such men could be found in Fynecountry. A few who could not mix pleasure with business; who would deny themselves – and their families - basic comforts in order to set an example of good leadership. On the other hand, what had it earned him? Really, what had it earned him? His two-bedroom flat, his old banger, few friends and (he was sure) an unhappy wife and child.

"Excuse me Sir, you must think I have an effrontery and it may be preposterous of me to think you will consider my suggestion, let alone change. But Sir, call me foolish, call me any name. But please Sir, listen to this. You say why waste in the midst of scarcity. I say, why suffer in the midst of plenty? Look at Professor Jantuzi in the Arts College. Do you know Dr. Aritzu in the College of Education in Gediu State? They are enjoying their position. Let me come nearer home Sir; our own Chief Atani. The man may have worked for some of his money, but not all. He uses people like you; and I'm sure has cut many corners here and there. That is life. He is enjoying his money; that is life. He is not stupid. Sir, life is to be enjoyed, and you only live it once."

"So are you saying I'm stupid not spending college money to buy a big house and flashy car?"

"No Sir, What I'm saying Sir, is that you take what rightly belongs to you. You are entitled to these comforts. Don't feel guilty claiming what is rightly yours .You seem scared to enjoy yourself. You are not doing Chief Atani a favour; in fact you are doing your family and us a big disfavour."

"What do you mean `us'? Who are you?

"You want to hear it? You want me to hit the nail on the head? We are your academic staff. You are blocking our way. As the man in charge, you are responsible for setting not only standards of discipline and academic achievement, but also standards of living….and I mean living well…. for us. Otherwise…" (he began to rise) "….get out, or we get you out!"

The boss sat still, wondering what had hit him. As he opened his mouth to speak, the young graduate assistant added. "Don't bother; I've seen all the reaction I want to see." He made for the door.

He went straight to the physics laboratory where his colleagues were; all senior staff, including the Deputy Provost who was that in name only, were eager to hear the result of the encounter. Unfortunately their emissary had little to report. When asked why he did not wait for his reaction, he replied, "I watched it, I enjoyed it, I did not need to hear it." Well said. Déjà vu. He heard it from his son; he heard it from his mother; he had just heard it from his staff; "Get out, or we get you out," the message echoed in his head. Another series of sleepless nights followed. He sincerely wished he could understand his people. Why could they not see life from his point of view?

****

He was the only different one in his family; and the most successful academically. The brother was now retired, after a meritorious service in the police force. Biletu remembered some scandal involving him a few years before his retirement; but it did not amount to much. Was it swept under the carpet just like many such acts by top officers? No not likely. His brother was also brought up in a Christian environment like him, but had little exposure to the outside world. The second brother studied Sociology at university, but decided to go into the imports and exports business. He believed every letter of live and let live, eat and let eat.

He was at home at every frontier and knew all customs officers by name. They in turn knew his stock-in-trade. Unfortunately he met an untimely death at a road block.

Stella, the only female in the family was one of the first groups of air hostesses for the national airline. She made extra money in contraband goods. It was a well-known secret that many air crews engaged in this activity; so she was not doing anything out of the ordinary. She was only buying and selling; not stealing. When Bintu was appointed headmistress, she encouraged her to look the part by bringing her new outfits from time to time. Her brother? Well, he could continue his miserly ways and earn himself a bad name. By the way, how about a woman-to-woman talk with Bintu? She would try it; at least the wife should know her husband better and might succeed in changing him.

Over the years, and contrary to what people believed, Bintu had come to love and respect her husband more. There was a secret and mutual admiration of each other, but no physical or outward show of it; he, out of pride; she out of fear and 'respect'. In Fynecountry culture, couples did not demonstrate love in public. Biletu supplied the basic necessities for the home; Junior's school fees were always paid promptly. Extras were provided by Bintu; both managed small monthly savings.

Bintu viewed her sister-in-law's discussion with suspicion. Was sister setting up sister-in-law?

"I know we were brought up to be good and honest in all things; but that era is gone. Life is for living now. Why should such an intelligent man who can easily make millions deny himself minimum luxury in the name of honesty? I can't understand my brother at all."

"I am sure my husband knows what he is doing; and honesty remains the best policy."

"Well, there are times when man's got to do what man's got to do; like you once did, remember?"

That did it. Bintu's suspicions were confirmed. This bitch's aim was not to help the brother but to humiliate her, and remind her of her past sins.

"Well, as you said, that era's gone. My husband and I dealt with it appropriately; and thank you for reminding me. You know what? Let's forget this topic. If indeed you want to help your brother, speak to him directly. Good day."

"I thought you could speak to him; but now I see you are also scared of him. Or maybe you are too comfortable in your own world, in your career, with your station wagon and driver, to worry about what happens to your husband. Anything we should know?"

"Yes. From now on I want you to leave us alone and mind your own business. You can keep your gifts because I can do without them." She swore to avoid her from then on.

****

Bintu's headship had a rocky start, but it soon stabilised in her favour. Her predecessor's transfer to another state was influenced by the present governor, who himself got the post through vote manipulation. The first term saw her trying to convince those she inherited that she was worth her salt. Since it was a staff school, priority was given to the university staff, junior and senior, while at the same time maintaining good standard. But she was finding it hard to refuse the brown envelopes from influential non-staff who wanted their children admitted. This was so tempting; the dilemma was not so much whether to succumb or not, but how to keep it from her husband. How would she handle all the extra cash without the risk of being accused of having an affair?

A great idea presented itself during one of her morning devotions. She would use the passage in Ephesians 4, verses 14-15 to break the ice and 'tell the truth in love'. Little did she know that her husband had similar plans in mind; a heart-to-heart discussion.

After a particularly turbulent night, Biletu decided to take the plunge. This would be a 'how's my driving?' type of talk. After all, a wedding anniversary was approaching.

Bintu welcomed the move, and listened; then "You tell me; how do you think we've done?"

"Well, could be better."

"It could be much better. Actually, I'm not worried for myself. What bothers me is Junior. He is growing up without much attention from his father. And of course your job; Junior says his friends used to call him the headmaster's son; now they call him the mote's son."

"Mote's son, why?"

"Well, a mote is something unpleasant; that must be removed. Isn't it?" She replied, recalling when she first applied this term to him.

Sure; he had delegated some powers to his deputy, and he was impressed with the way things were going. However it seemed that all the staff wanted was extra perks only illegal because they were not written down. As Koleson had bluntly pointed out, the provost should see to their 'welfare'. If he did not, they would see to it themselves.

Bintu remembered the early days when she considered her husband a mote in her eye that must be removed. Now she saw a veil over his eyes that needed removal.

"Let's face it; these gifts are …."

"You mean the brown envelopes?"

"How do you know they come in brown envelopes?"

"Many came my way while I was in the university."

"And what did you do with them?"

"They went back untouched. Even in the college; some came at first, but they soon stopped."

"Why?"

"Well, I made it clear I did not need them."

"You didn't need them!" exclaimed Bintu. "But they could have come handy all the time the car was in the garage; or when Junior needed new shoes; or when financial constraints stopped me from going for the special investigation the doctor recommended."

"What doctor? What investigation?"

"Forget that. I no longer need it any way. Let's stick to the 'brown envelopes' as you call them. From now on whoever enters my office with one is not going back with it. Moreover, I'm taking advantage of the university accommodation offered in my contract. We will soon need a bigger place. And while the going is good, I'm taking a car loan to get myself a personal car. Thomas has offered to give me driving lessons. He is one of the few drivers who actually went to driving school. So I trust him."

She had always been assertive. But since they came back together, Bintu had tried to be submissive: partly out of guilt and partly because she really wanted to make the marriage work. Nevertheless she was not going to forgo her comfort for either religion or morality. She knew that in some issues she had to take matters into her own hands. Such was the issue of an addition to the family. Biletu was contented with Junior as the only child, whilst Bintu would love a junior for Junior. So without consulting the husband she had sought the help of a doctor friend. At first she attributed her feeling of fatigue to stress and anxiety over her husband's job; but good news awaited her on her next visit to the doctor. She knew she had to break the news gently to the husband, who received it with indifference.

"Is that why you've been complaining of being tired lately? I attributed it to your job. You look radiant anyway." And after a pause, "I guess we have to start preparing for the new addition."

"Yes. As you know, hand-me-downs are out of the question; we also need more space and a reliable family car."

"Hmmm....we'll see."

9. Strange Encounter

Hakeem was noticeably absent from the staff meeting on Monday morning; it turned out he wasn't in at all. No word from him on Tuesday either. On Wednesday a note came from him through a young man on a motorcycle. Hakeem's son living with the grandmother in Ariba village had been knocked down by a stranger, driving a Mercedes Benz recklessly through the village path. Little Chineta was born to Hakeem while he was still in school, and was being looked after by his middle-aged mother. The driver would have been lynched by the villagers but for the quick intervention of a village elder. It turned out that the elder, Baba, as he was known, was the very man the owner-driver was visiting. He had brought some gifts to the father of his fiancée ahead of the impending traditional marriage ceremonies.

About an hour later, a small brown envelope was delivered to the boy's grandmother 'for some pain killers'. It contained one hundred mintos, just enough to buy a few tablets of paracetamol in the village chemist. The grandmother felt insulted and saddened by this, but could do nothing, since Baba was involved. News reached Hakeem later that the boy was having some abnormal movements soon after the accident; these later developed into full blown seizures.

In the village, Hakeem listened to the account of the incident. Was the old man's relationship with the stranger more important than his son's life? Or was it the fear of the stranger's tycoon father? He returned the brown envelope and its contents and paid the deposit to the village clinic where his son was being treated.

News of the incident soon spread to neighbouring villages and Baba was in trouble. Biletu could not believe his ears when he heard the full story and the identity of the offender. It was an opportunity for him to show his humane side and solidarity for his staff without being considered a coward. He too almost had a fit when he heard who the driver's father was, and that he was at the time abroad for medical check up and treatment. Chief Atani went on these trips at least twice a year to keep in good shape. Information had it that this particular son, the one after J-J, was once flown abroad to have a fracture mended. He sustained the fracture while playing football. Something flipped in Biletu and he went into action.

Koleson and Tamara, two members of staff known for their boldness and love of excitement, were told emergency situation demanded emergency solution. The college accountant was taken aback by the authority behind the order for him to sign some documents, which he did without much questioning. The two spent the whole day out and came back with a brand new station wagon marked 'Office of the Provost' and a mini bus marked 'College of Sciences Staff Bus'. The latter was immediately sent to help Hakeem back with Chineta. In the meantime, Biletu went to a nearby private clinic to set up a retainer's account for the college staff and family. Chineta was the first patient.

Back in Ariba village, Baba was scolded by fellow elders, and they vowed to boycott the wedding ceremony. Unfortunately the little boy passed away ten days after the incident.

Chief Atani was away longer than expected. Some test results were taking longer than usual, people were told. Instead of apologies, Hakeem's family received threats and warning to desist from tarnishing the good name of the Atani family. Arrangements were made for security forces to make the impending event hitch-free. Hakeem's family could only watch with disbelief and much hurt .The college staff were well represented at the funeral. Some went in their private cars, while the rest travelled in the new official cars.

The date for the traditional wedding came and went; there was no sign of the Chief. Rumours started flowing about his health, and different diseases were trumped up. In Ariba village many prayed he die of the 'mouth-to-foot disease' he contracted abroad.

10. The Eye Opener

The Provost left early for his office in the new official car. He was greeted outside the building by two men who showed him their I D cards. Their mission was to arrest him for drug-related offences. Although they spoke fluent English, they were obviously French nationals. Thinking he could better help them in their search by speaking their mother tongue, he resorted to his knowledge of the language. They were not impressed.

He was given a few minutes to lock the car before they half pushed him into their own car.

From the local police station he was driven all the way to Lebon. As he was being led into a cell, he caught sight of some known faces; among them Philip his accountant, and Rev. Dafid. They were in separate cells. The only common denomination among them he could figure out was the college; but what about it? Had some staff been growing cannabis in the lab? Were students dealing in drugs?

News of the arrest sent Bintu into premature labour. With Tamara's help she was taken to the hospital where their thirty-four-week-gestation baby girl was born. The midwife, who she knew from Church, complained bitterly about the disturbance to their peaceful sleep by an early raid to the house next door where the man was taken away on suspicion of being involved in drug trafficking.

"Poor man," she said. "And his wife was not even at home; she travels abroad from time to time on business."

Bintu thought it wise not to mention her husband's arrest as well. She felt helpless where she lay, cuddling the new arrival. Her husband's innocence was unquestionable. His offence, if any, was naivety.

Biletu was released two days later, no wiser as to the reason for his arrest. He was given a free ride back, as the officers had other arrests to make in the region. Before he leant back to catch up on his sleep, one of his escorts said they hoped that the lack of sleep opened his eyes and the mosquitoes his ears. The new release did not get the message; or the joke.

He was overjoyed with the new baby who he immediately named Gloria, to Bintu's relief.

The only news he had was the sighting of Philip and the Reverend Dafid. Still no one could come up with the connection.

"Poor fellows," he muttered.

Thursday's edition of The Vendor carried some news about the Chief's whereabouts. He had been detained by the Interpol on charges connected with drug trafficking. One of his couriers was a woman, whose husband, a college accountant, was also under arrest. A paragraph mentioned the arrest and release of the provost of the College of Sciences, one of the Chief's assets. The article also alluded to the fact that the college was one of his 'fronts', with some of his associates on the Board. How this was possible was beyond Biletu's imagination. Obviously his ears and eyes were still not open. He called a meeting to appeal to his staff to try to carry on their various assignments as best as they could.

Just as he was leaving the staff meeting, two bounced cheques were presented to him. They were from the car dealer in town. Biletu concluded the college assets must have been frozen. How could the government do that without consulting him, or without consideration for the day-to-day running of such an institution? "Any way this is Fynecountry," he concluded, as if that was any consolation.

It was far from being a consolation to the students who through their union came up with various demands of their own; among them a students' bus. Through their union leader they presented a plan by which a revolving fund (the college must be rich) would yield some financial benefits to them. No one in the college administration would be involved. They could not be trusted. The students would manage the fund themselves.

11. Serious Encounter

Biletu knew he had heard the voice at the other end of the phone before, but could not immediately identify it. "It's John Bull." said the voice. A meeting was arranged.

John Bull, a good friend in his university days and a fellow Crabster, had an accounting firm a few miles away. It was he who opened Biletu's eyes to the true finances of his college. According to the ledger for the office of the provost, the latter purchased a station wagon for official use and a Mercedes Benz for his personal use right at the opening of the college. Each vehicle had a driver paid by the college. A ledger claimed that there were two student buses, while another one had documents purporting the details of a lump sum borrowed by the college for car loans. The dates of the latter did not tally with the official ones for a few members after the staff protest. John Bull looked at his friend. "You are in big trouble."

"That can't be right. I did not know this was going on."

"Exactly; you have to explain your ignorance of all this mess, which, I'm afraid, won't be easy."

"How about the bounced cheques; the guy wants his money."

"Don't worry about that. The car company is part of Atani's assets. So it's a small fraction of the people's money coming back to the people."

"John, how do you know all this?"

"My name is John Bull. I am alive and well and living in Fynecountry, not in Cuckoo Land."

Words failed his visitor. After a pause, he said "Please help; for old times' sake."

John was willing to help; but it was a big job for which he knew his friend could not pay.

"I will help; but not for nothing." This was a big break for his company both in income and in fame. He had friends in the media houses as well.

His friend sat there helpless. "Look, don't be so daft. The job will pay for itself by the time we finish; the money is there within the ledgers. We know our job. You were hand-picked for your job; and you must have done it well for them to have gone this far."

He didn't ask who he was referring to; after all his eyes and ears were supposed to be opening.

"Before I leave, can I ask why you came to my help? I mean…apart from the money?"

"Papa Cletus is my uncle."

Biletu thanked his friend and left.

****

Ben was Baba's oldest son, and according to tradition, had an influence in family matters. He had never hidden his opposition to the union of Atani family and his; but his sister was adamant. The ill feelings dated back to when the Chief referred to him as 'the village boy' when he was dating the Chief's second cousin, who later married Philip. Like many others, Ben had always been aware of the Chief's nefarious activities. And there were times when he was tempted to blow the whistle from his foreign base; but after all, some citizens were benefiting from the proceeds. One of them was the college. However with the Chineta case, the family fell deep into the trap. Through his remote control, Ben got the baron arrested leaving an Italian restaurant in London with his cousin-cum-courier, Philip's wife.

J-J was able to pay top lawyers to defend his brother in court. There was no post-mortem to prove that the seizures were as a result of the collision with the car. In any case the journey from the village to Olito could have worsened the boy's condition and caused his death. The verdict was misadventure.

Gloria's first Church attendance saw Biletu in Church again. He wasn't quite sure what his offering was for; the opportunity of the ordeal to open his eyes and ears, or for coming through it alive. What he did not realise was that it could have been much worse. Philip and the rest were still being held since they could not produce the cash being demanded by the police for their release. The law of the land did not define who the thief was: the blatant robber or the law-enforcer hiding behind the law.

12. Friends or Foes

Six months after Chief Atani's disappearance, J-J requested a meeting with the Provost. He was sorry for the havoc wreaked by his father's detractors. He was sure all would soon be over and his good name restored. (Biletu didn't know what to make of the bluff). The incident with the little boy was unfortunate; but he should not have been allowed to play ball into the village path. His brother could not have been speeding; hence the boy didn't sustain any scratch or immediate effect. (This was from J-J who studied science at university and was desperate to study medicine). What did the Provost think of the take-over bid by the federal government? Would he be interested in forming a consortium to rescue the college?

Biletu thought for a minute; "Come back in a few weeks; I'll have my answer." Wise man.

****

Four men and a woman sat at the round table to discuss proposals for the new venture.

"The purpose of this company is …."

"Sorry. Are we here for a company or a college?" Biletu cut in.

"We are forming a consortium - call it company if you will - to manage the college. We…"

"This is new to me. Please go easy with me. I'm more familiar with laboratories, pipettes, and Bunsen burners."

"That's obvious," replied John Bull, the chairman of the meeting, "and that's why we're here to rescue you." Rescue indeed!

Since the earlier surprise contact with Biletu, John Bull had certainly been of tremendous help in exposing and rectifying massive fraud in the college accounts. He also made good money for himself. More importantly he saw in the trend of events an opportunity for more and more power and money. That was the purpose of the meeting.

Unlike his friend the academician, he knew the whereabouts of many old friends. Hence he was able to muster their goodwill. All except the woman were old crabsters.

"Looks like the poor crabs have come back to haunt us," joked one.

"The aphrodisiac has worked wonders by my reckoning," said another.

"Yes. It sure did some good; some havoc as well."

"I don't know what you guys are talking about; I thought we were here for some serious matter."

It was the woman's voice.

According to the plan which unfolded, each member would be a financier, investing an agreed amount which, together with the existing assets of the college, would form 'the fund'. Biletu would of course continue as the provost; Jo knew a reliable friend who would deal with the legal matters; John Bull knew a host of accountants; the woman was a PR expert.

Biletu was wise enough to make notes of all that was being said. He was not going to agree to anything without the counsel of his wife.

Bintu had often boasted of having Xray eyes. Those eyes saw through every aspect of the plan.

"Where are you going to get the money to invest, may I ask? They are not talking of your kind of pocket money you know. Your friends are already company directors with a lot of cash to spare. This is going to be part-time for them. Wake up, and break the curse."

"What curse?"

"The curse of being used as door mat."

"Now that you mention curse; I wonder if I was indeed cursed because I broke a link of chain letters?"

"What chain? What letters?"

"Remember when we were young we used to send some letters round purporting them to be from some divine power and asking that they be passed on indefinitely. Well I remember breaking one because they were too many, and I didn't really believe they were for real."

Bintu didn't know whether to laugh or cry at this child-ish reply. But the husband looked serious; so she continued; "Darling, these people are too smart for you."

"I voiced my concern about not having the money; Jo offered me a loan from the Marine Bank where he is manager." (Another urge to laugh).

"And whose pocket will you be lining by so doing? Moreover, do you know that the woman, Mary, is Jo's sister?"

"How do you know?"

"She's in my Fellowship meeting. Through her some members got mortgage from the Marine Bank. Can't you see you are the odd one out? The poorest, the most naïve, the easiest to con. You will be squeezed out before you know it."

"What should I do?"

"Pull out now. Tell them you are not for the consortium; you'd rather the Federal Government take it over. I mean the Federal, not State government. The latter is too close for comfort."

"But how can friends do this to me? We were all friends in......"

"Forget that. That was years ago. In today's Fynecountry only the fit can be rich and only the very rich can survive. The bottom line is, frankly, one cannot survive on pocket money only."

"Are you saying we cannot survive for much longer?"

"Answer that question yourself. Junior will soon be in secondary school, we need more money when Gloria starts nursery. Cost of living is soaring. How can you not see the problem?"

"What do you suggest I do with Bunsen burners and pipettes?"

"Give me the go-ahead. Even the acids and alkalis will work wonders."

"Does the Bible not say that the love of money is the root of all evil?" Biletu knows that passage very well.

Bintu on her part remembered her morning devotion for that day. "Encourage him and strengthen him," God instructed Moses with regards to Joshua's leadership of the children of Israel. She was sure the message in Deuteronomy was for their situation.

"No," she answered; "not in all cases. Not when the need necessitates it. After all, we can't steal. Don't worry, I'll look through your microscopes and see a way. God will make a way."

The 'amen' was hardly audible.

"Like Prophet Ezekiel breathed on the dry bones, I will breathe on those lifeless glass tubes and pipettes and they will come alive and serve us."

By this time, Biletu was no longer listening.

It was Hakeem who brought hot news after the weekend. Chief Atani's daughter-in-law to-be had fled the country. There were conflicting stories as to her whereabouts. Some said she had fled with another man; while others claimed she was with her brother at his foreign base. Even Baba did not know where she was hiding; nor did he understand why she had to hide. In any case J-J and family were demanding a refund of all gifts, cash and kind: not because they could not forgo the items, but to force the girl out of hiding. It was a big showdown for Baba on Saturday, with no support from the rest of the village.

Other members of staff had been following news about the rest of the detainees. Those who attended the same Church as Rev. Dafid told how he gave testimony of his release. He related how he and his friends (in crime) were like Paul and Silas in the Bible. They prayed and sang day and night; then one day out of the blue, their release was announced. The congregation burst into songs and dance and gave generously into the large thanksgiving bowls going round. After the service the local Chief Police Officer congratulated him on his brilliant testimony.

The news of the take-over of the college was welcome by the students, who saw more comfort and advantages coming their way, to be at par with the university not too far away. The students' centre was always agog with activists preparing their demands. Cletus, now an undergraduate, was the newly-elected leader.

13. Mysterious Work of Man

The provost was just starting to doze off after marking some examination scripts when he was awakened by loud banging on his door. A group of students had brought the news of a fire in the chemistry and physics laboratories. It was bad. The only fire engine was out on an earlier call. The one from miles away was on its way. In the meantime students were using buckets of water to tackle the blaze; but the oxygen cylinders were fuelling the conflagration. Biletu jumped into the car while the wife went on her knees.

What he saw, even in the dark, was beyond description. The fire engine arrived as the roof was crumbling; nothing was worth risking a life for. They could only make sure that all embers were completely extinguished. There was no doubt that arsonists had been at work. There were sightings of shadowy figures running from the scene. A group was heard the night before discussing 'the plan'. Someone saw Cletus acting suspiciously around the laboratories about half an hour before the alarm was raised. It was difficult to pinpoint a motive on anyone other than the Atani family. But whodunnit?

Biletu fought back tears as he surveyed the devastation. Who could have done this wicked act?

A few days later a team of investigators arrived from the Federal Ministry to look into the matter, make proposals for immediate rebuilding of new laboratories and arrangements for the release of funds. Pastor Alfred was the second-in-command in the team.

Biletu was impressed with the speed at which things moved. Moreover he was given free hand to employ builders and suppliers of furniture items. Being a novice at such activities, he went about asking his staff to introduce bricklayers and handy men of sorts. He narrowly escaped the bucket of hot water Bintu was holding when he told her what he was doing. He wanted to spoil the mysterious wonders of God.

Had he never heard of contracts? Had he never heard of tenders? "Man! God is throwing good cash onto your laps and you are brushing it off. This is the time for an influx of brown envelopes."

"But I can't give every one of them a job."

"It is a risk they are prepared to take. And don't think that they will give you money they can't afford. They are not stupid."

He spent the rest of the evening taking lessons from his astute wife. She would keep an account of the 'income'. Despite Bintu's effort, Biletu was still not convinced he could match his wife's expectation; but an event was about to change things.

****

Since the birth of Gloria and the purchase of the official car, Biletu felt more comfortable making occasional visits to the village. On his arrival one Sunday morning, the Church service was still on; so he sat down reluctantly in the back row and listened to the sermon on man and mammon. What a coincidence! He left Church thinking that was the best sermon he had ever listened to and that it was specifically for him. The preacher started with Matt.6:24 in which Jesus warned against serving mammon; that is riches. He went on to contrast this with Luke 16:9-11 in which Jesus advised His disciples to 'make friends with the unrighteous mammon for the rainy day'. He then linked these two passages to Ecclesiastes 7:12---"wisdom is a defence, and money is a defence"---to show that money had always been recognised as important, a defence against poverty. The key message, according to the preacher, was not to serve or worship riches; but to let riches serve them.

"Yes!" thought Biletu. "It has come from the horse's mouth. Even the Bible acknowledges the importance of money. Now I believe Bintu. We need money, and we shall make it; plenty of it." Back home, he discussed his latest experiences which even his wife found incredible. What coincidence; no doubt the message was for them.

Before the laboratories resumed full operation, Biletu took two trips abroad; all paid for by the government, to buy authentic equipment and chemicals, mostly reagents. He bought enough for both the college and the supply store which he had quickly opened. The money was coming in so fast he could not believe his luck. The mysterious work of God!

He made frequent visits to the village to inspect and leave money for the four-bedroom house he was erecting; again thanks to Bintu and her acumen. Charles had offered to oversee the day-to-day activities for free; but Biletu insisted on paying him token sums from time to time.

His members of staff were not left out of Biletu's change of heart and outlook; more relaxed and approachable. Few were aware of his private business because he still gave his academic work priority.

14. Fynecountry Style

The Bonsala family were seen together more in public and putting up a united front.

Biletu was the obvious choice as Chairman at Koleson's wedding reception. A few days to the time, he was seen brushing down one of his nice suits. "You are not wearing that to the wedding, are you?" exclaimed Bintu.

"Why not?" replied the husband.

"You should look the part," said the wife. "Don't worry, I will fix everything. It is a big occasion which your staff will attend; and who knows, some dignitaries as well."

True to her word, Bintu did not disappoint. Having been to a few of such weddings, mainly of her staff and Fellowship members, she knew how the chairman was expected to look like, and the protocol of the chairman's speech.

"I can hardly recognise myself," Biletu said, looking in the mirror.

"I recognise you. You look handsome, rich and like a chairman. You look like you should look when going to a wedding, not to a lecture."

Normally he would have asked for an explanation of the last sentence, but he just laughed. On the whole he felt good.

The wedding was an outing of some sort; a statement of his 'arrival'. The acknowledgement was obvious. The handshakes, words of greetings, of approval, of commendation; all gave the same message: he was now doing what he should have been doing. In his chairman's speech he even made a joke about Koleson's promise to 'get him out'. The bridegroom had indeed succeeded in getting him out in an unusual way to his wedding.

The best part was the dancing. He watched as the new couple opened the floor, bombarded by friends and relatives cheering and throwing minto bills of different denominations at them. Two young girls were in attendance gathering them into bags. Biletu's heart started to beat fast. He had conformed this far and received admiration; how would he tackle this next phase? He had no money on him; certainly not as much as he had seen people throwing at the couple.

He shouldn't have worried, with his wife beside him. She gave him a nudge and handed him a brown envelope. As if on cue, he heard his name over the loudspeaker as the next to dance. The next rendition by the dance band was in his and his wife's honour. He was a learned man, the best provost in the country, and the husband any woman would wish for. Above all, he was an eminent and generous member of society, the Managing Director of Biletu Laboratories. (The chairman missed a step). Bintu, the song went on, was an elegant woman, a worthy and stalwart wife, an honest headmistress who was doing the staff school proud. In the meantime the two were displaying their wealth as they were supposed to do. Bintu had no problem displaying the latest dance steps whilst the husband could only manage those popular in his student days. The applause was deafening and Biletu found himself relaxing and actually enjoying the afternoon.

Among his rhetorical questions on their way home were, how 'those boys' knew about his chemicals business? How did they come about the title of Managing Director? He never called or considered himself that. "It felt good though."

When he got home from work on Monday he announced to his wife , "You know, people seem to think of me differently now that we have money. Someone referred to me as chairman this morning. So I reckon I'm now Dr. Provost Chairman Managing Director Biletu Bonsala."

"That sounds nice," Bintu said.

"Ridiculous. Utter nonsense," replied the husband.

"Enjoy it while it lasts."

A few such outings followed in quick succession, with Bintu having to 'dress' her husband up for the occasions. Each also demanded lavish display of wealth. Even Bintu became bewildered at the way things were going. They were at a dilemma as to which invitation to accept and which to reject, not wanting to offend anyone.

Bintu had not forgotten her own ambition while helping her husband to become popular. She assured him she had put aside enough money to rent a house not too far from the university to start her own private nursery school. She gave a number of reasons why she preferred this to her present job; top on the list was, of course, more money. It was difficult for the husband to object, although at the back of his mind he feared they were heading for more than they bargained for.

In the months that followed, he was called upon to donate to charity funds, the origin and aims of which he did not quite understand. He wished he knew what was happening to the donations.

Charles proved to be a trustworthy friend and monitored the progress of the house in the village closely. During one of Biletu's visits, Charles called him aside for a private talk.

"There's a chieftaincy title going in the village; and we think you are the most appropriate person for it." Charles disclosed.

"Count me out!" was the angry reply.

"But we need people like you to do the village proud; to raise the status, and contribute financially to its progress."

Financially! He had hardly made the money before demands on it came pouring in. That was proof that joining them was a big mistake.

Bintu was of course in favour of such title, but the husband was adamant. Deep down he felt uncomfortable because he knew many warmed up to him not because they were true friends but because they now saw him as one of them; doing what was right by their standards.

Going back or opting out was not easy.

That was in the social aspect of life in Fynecountry. He hadn't yet broken into the religious circle.

Gloria's christening was an opportunity for this, and Bintu wasn't going to let it slip by. Apart from the Church congregation, the list she compiled included friends and celebrities. To Biletu's greatest surprise and chagrin, the godfather was to be J.J. Atani.

"What on earth has come upon you? Are you out of your mind?"

Bintu went on to reveal that J.J. was one of the new recruits into the Fellowship at the last meeting. He had confided in her that he was trying to make a come-back into the limelight in Olito and the region in general, after the embarrassment of the father's arrest and the saga that followed. The name of the family had been tarnished and business was not thriving as usual. Former clients did not want to be seen as accomplices. A deep sigh from the husband was the reply. J.J. even confided in her that he was glad the federal government took over the college. Although he was close to his father, he was not brave enough to discuss his nefarious dealings with him. In fact he had to pretend he did not know about it. He had thought of going for further studies so as to become an academic, but he was not really cut out for that. He preferred business.

"He was very frank with me; and I feel we should help him."

"I will agree to this if you can answer my questions. Why you? Why us? In what way will my daughter's christening help to 'launch' J.J. or the Atani family?"

"Well, I guess he still respects you as his old school teacher. He knows I'm influential in religious circles; which could be a bonus in our society. Many important personalities will be at the christening to see him, and possibly his father."

"That does not guarantee a change of heart; in fact it can backfire on us."

"I'm sure they will yield. Are we all not actors on the same stage? Once he starts mixing in the right circles, he'll be all right. He just needs the 'launching' as you call it. After all Barnabas had to launch Paul before the rest of the disciples could trust him, because of his past."

Biletu couldn't agree more. Was he not being 'launched' as well?

"Don't tell me Philip's wife is going to be the godmother."

"No. I promise."

The two new converts performed their roles very well; Biletu in Church during offertory and special thanksgiving, J.J. at the reception that followed.

Since Biletu had restricted his reagents business to bulk supplies, it was easy for him to keep tabs on his accounts. He created two budgets; the old and normal one he called the salary budget, the other one the business budget. The latter had the income and the lifestyle sections. The expenditure was so named because that was exactly what it was used for--- the new lifestyle .He soon discovered that, while the actual gain was substantial, there was hardly anything left after the expenditure. For any real gains he would have to increase prices. For Biletu that was too much and unreasonable. Why should innocent people at the end of the equation pay for his unwarranted lifestyle? His conscience went out to the average parents who would have to pay higher laboratory fees or whatever name their institution gave to the use of their science equipment. While he truly appreciated the exposure to the real life in his beloved country, he did not think he could cope much longer at that pace. He knew people travelled abroad for periods of respite; but that cost money too. What had he let himself into?

He was still having this dilemma when Bintu came home one day to announce that she had nominated him to be the Church harvest chairman in two months' time.

"And how much would I be expected to donate?"

"Well, last year's chairman gave fifty thousand mintos; I'm sure you could do better than that. To whom much is given much is expected."

He walked away to prevent himself from strangling her. As if possessed, she went after him. "God has opened your door to wealth; you have to keep the doors of His house open."

"At the moment the door is only ajar; pray that the door be opened wide so I can go in to bring out the big money."

"Give in faith to ask for more. Faith is evidence of things not seen."

"I can't remember you mentioning parties and Church donations when you said we needed more money. I only heard bigger accommodation, children's school fees and our comfort."

"Do not hide your light under the bushel. The whole society must know you've been blessed."

It was hard to determine who had the greater gift of repartee.

Bintu took the opportunity to remind the husband how useful her private nursery school would be. Biletu was in no mood to discuss it.

15. Mysterious Work Of Mammon

He was helping Junior with his homework when a car pulled up outside his house. The occupant who emerged from the back seat was well known to Biletu, only of much slimmer frame than his old self. Chief Atani straightened out the creases in his attire and walked head high to the gate.

"What have I done to deserve this?" thought Biletu. In any case he welcomed the visitor with hugs and handshake and offered him one of his new armchairs. The chief sat down looking around and wondering at the sparse and mediocre furniture in the provost's accommodation. Little did he know that what he was seeing was far better than what he would have seen had he visited some months earlier.

He asked after the rest of the family, congratulated him on the new addition, and the beautiful laboratory. The takeover by the Federal Government was wrong; but he was not going to contest it since it was still serving its purpose for the youths of the country. His recent experience had shown him a strange side of his people; they did not love him, only his money. Even those whom he had helped in the past now shied away from him. He feared not only for himself but also for his sons. J.J. was struggling to keep the family businesses going, as well as his personal matters which were not doing too well either. "And that story about my son Michael; envious people just wove untrue stories around the poor guy. I heard the young boy died of seizures, and his family just wanted money for his burial."

Biletu could not contain his anger any longer. "Hold it!" he said angrily. "That boy happened to be the son of one of my staff. How could you say they just wanted money off you? Your son drove carelessly through the village, with no regard for the little ones playing in their surroundings; knocked one down, as a result of which he suffered head injuries and subsequently seizures. If your son had been sensible and caring, immediate treatment would have saved the poor boy's life. Instead, he insulted the family by sending money for paracetamol. You are worrying about losing your businesses; some innocent life had been lost."

The chief held his head in his hands and looked genuinely sorry. He swore he was going by the story he was told; so he just concluded that was another way to get at his family. He promised to see Hakeem as soon as possible.

The main reason for his visit was to share with him some of his experiences during his absence.

The host could not help wondering what qualified him for this privilege. Did he think he was still an idiot? Anyway, baring one's mind after such an ordeal could be therapeutic; so he would lend a listening ear. By this time the chief was half way through the bottle of cold beer Biletu had put before him. Chances were he would need another one, if not a few more. The beer belly needed revival.

His story was a mixture of lies, half truths, and arrogance. The chief was surprised that only he and his close associates were arrested; it was a cover-up to save the necks of the others; others whose names he would not mention, but who God in His own good time would expose. He wasn't actually in prison in the UK as rumours carried it; a Church organisation gave him accommodation and everyone was nice to him. Stories carried in the local newspapers about him being Her Majesty's guest were all lies. He was safe in the hands of God's people. By the way, could Biletu remember his prayer at the gathering of the college officials, when he said that God moved in mysterious ways to perform His wonders? Well, his arrest abroad and stay with the religious people was God's way of calling him to serve Him. He spent most of the time studying the Bible in preparation for the next phase of his life to which the Lord had called him. During one of the devotional services, the Lord laid it in his heart to serve Him on his return home; that and only that would prove his gratitude to his maker. Biletu checked the bottle he had placed in front of the chief to make sure it wasn't a bottle of wine he was downing.

The visitor wasn't finished yet. He had made a mistake. No. Many of them had made this mistake; but only a few, he among them, were chosen in this miraculous way to serve God. He felt privileged. What blasphemy, thought Biletu.

"You see," continued the visitor; "our society is very funny...."

"Tell me about it," thought Biletu.

"I was quite comfortable; my guest house business was yielding enough for me to be able to send my children to good schools and give them higher education as well. But people thought I was very rich and started demanding from me more than I could afford. So I had no choice but to look for other ways to match their expectations."

Now Biletu felt insulted. "Of course you had a choice. You could have ignored them, or just give what you could afford."

"It's not that easy. When you have a chieftaincy title and everyone sings your praises wherever you go, you feel obliged to please. And once in, it's difficult to get out. Believe me; I sought ways, but found none. And what I did seemed innocent enough."

"If we are talking of the same crime, you have to show me the meaning of the word 'innocent' in your dictionary."

"Oh come on, you can't call that a crime. Those who need it will die unless they get it. In fact I was told my supply saved a life."

The listener, even though a chemist, knew little about those illegal drugs and their trafficking; nor was he interested in knowing. So he ignored what he just said, doubting his sanity.

"Anyway to return to the present and more important issue, we may have gone astray in the eyes of the law, but God Himself has thought it fit to use me to spread His word."

Biletu noticed the change in the pronoun from singular to plural and back to singular. What an escape from reality and responsibility for his misdeeds!

Just then the chief reached for his brief case and started fiddling inside. A gun! Biletu was about to dive to the floor when the hand reappeared holding a Bible.

"The next phase of my life therefore is based on Habakkuk chapter 2 verse 14. At this point he asked his host if he had a Bible and to bring it out so they could deliberate on the word of God.

He was surprised at the promptness with which Biletu produced one and opened the passage which read:

For the earth shall be filled

With the knowledge of the glory of the Lord

As the waters cover the sea

"So what?"

"So the word of God has to be spread wide and deep as the waters of the sea."

"So what? I still don't see your point. Have you come to spread the word to me?"

"What I'm saying is, while I was away…"

"Behind bars," Biletu almost added.

".….the Lord laid it in my heart while we were studying this passage that He would like me to be among those to spread His word throughout the world."

"So do it. After all you go to Church. You just have to be more active and maybe preach once in a while; spread the gospel."

"He wants me to do more than that; He wants me to start a new Church."

"I don't have the money to lend you to build a Church; nor can I ever be a member of your Church."

"That's not it."

Biletu's mind went to J.J. using the Fellowship as a saving platform. Bintu was an active member of the Fellowship. Did the chief also want to use his wife? As he opened the second bottle of beer, he hit the nail on the head. Could his learned friend allow him the use of the big lecture hall as the meeting place for his religious group?

"And I guess you have a pastor-in-waiting in J.J.?"

"No. J.J. has some business ideas of his own." Business; was that a slip of tongue?

"Before we leave Habakkuk; did you deliberate on only verse 14?"

The smart provost would not be fooled. Bintu must have 'deliberated' on the same passage at some point because several verses of the chapter had been highlighted.

"Verses 15 speaks of a curse on those who give others dangerous substances to warp their minds. And if you understood verses 16 and 17, you would not have considered your business innocent."

"Judge not so ye shall not be judged," was the reply.

"Well, good luck in your new venture. With J.J's background, there's a business I'm sure he'll be interested in." Some coughing came from the kitchen. It was Bintu who had been eavesdropping. She could see the husband treading on dangerous grounds.

"He has thought of teaching; he can't do it so forget it."

"It's not teaching. Just ask him to see me on Thursday morning in my office. As for the use of a hall in the college, I'll let you know which one you can use. But for a fee."

As soon as Chief Atani left, Bintu came out to warn the husband of any dealings with the chief. Had he forgotten his ordeal so soon? Did he want the society to shun them as they were doing to the Atanis? Greater shock was yet to come for Bintu.

****

At exactly 11o'clock on Thursday morning, J.J.'s knock on the provost's door was answered by the secretary who assured him that her boss was indeed expecting him. Memories of yesteryears flashed through both minds as he went in and sat down in front of his former lecturer. Now it was like a job interview. The older man could feel the tension. He had planned to ask him about his plans to become a pastor in his father's Church, but he changed his mind and quickly put the poor guy at ease.

Going straight to the point, he told him of this small business enterprise; it was already established and doing well. There was great opportunity for growth and expansion but it needed devotion and business acumen which was why the present owner was looking for someone who would give it all it deserved; in other words, someone to buy the business.

J.J. sat back in his chair and thought for a moment.

"What sort of business is it?"

"It is a business supplying laboratory equipment and reagents. At the moment it deals with bulk supplies to hospitals, universities, colleges, private laboratories etc. It is recognised as a trusted and reliable source of various reagents; there's quality assurance, and expiry dates are respected; unlike the other sources. If well managed, is will yield good returns. Another advantage is that these establishments either need the goods or they don't. There's little contact between you and them as long as you fulfil your terms of business. It's mainly paper work."

"It sounds too good to be true. Why would anyone want to part with such business?"

"As I said, holding on to it is like wasting an opportunity or hiding a lamp under a bushel."

"What if this is a ruse? Do you know the present owner well, and have you got proof of the existence of these reagents?"

"Very well; and full proof."

"I will be interested if the price is right; and of course I need information about the original sources for future purchases and expansion like you said."

"No problem."

The visit to the storeroom was fixed for the following day.

The young man could not believe his eyes. It was obvious who owned the business. Both men went through relevant documents, including addresses of laboratories abroad, contacts, price lists, etc. Biletu made sure he did not hold back any information that would help the young entrepreneur. Neither did he hold back the true reason why he wanted to sell it, despite its bright prospects.

"Did your father ever discuss his recent experiences and predicament with you?"

"No"

"Without going into details, he admitted he had enough money for good and decent family life.

But social circumstances and expectations forced him to look for ways to fuel the lifestyle he found himself in and more importantly, to please people. After his return, the same people did not want to know him."

"Yes that's true; most of his friends now avoid him. They claim under-cover policemen and women are watching his movements; which is not true."

"My boy, you know me very well. But things happened to me I felt I had to prove I was no fool; that I could make money if I wanted to. However I soon discovered it only brought unwanted attention, false friends, and misery. I found I was making money, not for my family to enjoy but for others in order to gain false recognition. It became a millstone round my neck. I want to go back to my old self; if I don't need it, I don't need to make it."

A deep sigh from J.J.

"Don't worry. You are still young .You need money to establish yourself. But save for the rainy day." His thoughts went back to those days when, even though a hard working student, he was being pushed beyond his limits; his heart went out to him. The former teacher-turned-mentor agreed to sell off the remaining stock and transfer ownership to his former student-turned-businessman for a sum that would leave him a handsome gain after paying off his rent of the store. Both parted happy associates.

He had transferred the millstone onto another neck; one he was convinced could bear the weight.

16. Daddy Is Not Well

"That was a good party; don't you think?" Bintu said to the husband on their way back from Esther's 40th birthday party. "I must ask her for the details of the band; boy, were they good!"

"I bet they cost an arm and a leg."

"Maybe; but we are up to it, honey. The entrance exams are coming; and so will some brown envelopes."

"Lucky you."

"The reagents will contribute their quota as well; add colour to the occasion."

"Dream on," said the husband to himself.

All this was about Bintu's approaching 40th birthday celebration. It would be a knock-out! The money had to be generated.

After an uncomfortable silence, Bintu continued; "You are tired, I see. I suggested we take Thomas, but you said no. He would have been glad to make a few mintos."

"The poor guy needs time with his family at weekends, not drive the boss round to her parties."

The rest of the journey was quiet.

Throughout the following week, while Bintu spent her free time noting down 'to-dos', for her party, Biletu had only one, a difficult one; to tell the wife to go easy, because the reagents would not be contributing any quota. He thought of different strategies, even employing the help of Junior. Was the store house burgled? Was it burnt down? These were too blatant. Maybe the government closed it down. No; such action would be in the local and national newspapers.

Yes! He punched the air when the idea occurred to him. He would get the buyer himself to do the job. He called on J.J. to find out how he was getting on. Were all the contacts cooperating? How was he getting used to the idea of being in big business again?

"There's one big favour I'd like you to do for me." Not waiting for any reaction, he continued; "My wife does not yet know that the business has been sold---to you. She would have a fit if I told her. She was actually instrumental in starting it, and has built so much hope on it. Now it's gone, I need to tell her."

The young man could not understand why his erstwhile dreaded lecturer was not brave enough to break such news to his wife. However J.J. agreed to give testimony of the Lord's miraculous answer to prayer at the next Fellowship meeting; how God had used His beloved, His anointed Mrs. Bintu Bonsala to answer one of his greatest desires. He now owned a reagents business; the much coveted one that supplied reliable goods to laboratories far and near.

"At the last but one meeting, we deliberated on faith in God, and how He could send help from the most un-expected quarters. Well, it's happened to me. Dr. Bonsala has transferred ownership of the business to me." J.J. testi-fied at the meeting. The shouts of 'Praise the Lord!' filled the air. Caroline, who was leading the meeting, started a chorus to which everyone danced; everyone except Bintu who was shocked beyond words. But she quickly managed to compose herself and made some awkward movements as if joining in the dance.

Meanwhile at home Biletu knew what was in store for him, and took measures to soften the impact. On the coffee table in front of him were spread out packets of malaria tablets, paracetamol, anti-diarrhoea, analgesia, anti-emetic medication, and some liniment. Junior was beside him rub-bing his back while he was fanning himself. The young one looked really upset and appeared to have been crying.

"Daddy is not well; he says I should keep the lights dim because bright lights upset him," were Junior's welcoming words to his mother. "Our teacher says that bright lights and noise can irritate the brain and can cause convulsions; so daddy needs peace and quiet."

Bintu scanned through the medications before the hus-band. "Well, he'd better look for the anticonvulsant because he's going to need it." Pushing the husband's head from his hands she shouted, "And what are you now, godfather or Father Christmas, or guardian angel or what?"

Biletu put his head back in his hands without looking up.

"You are just a foolish man; one without foresight one without backbone, one without feelings for his family, one without any love for the wife; one with poverty written across his forehead. Yes you should hide your head in shame."

"Peace and quiet be unto you," whispered Biletu, cynically. He was determined to frustrate his wife into submission. After all she would never see his point of view.

Bintu went on into the night on how the husband who 'knew nothing but books' mismanaged a lucrative business; she could have done better. In any case she did not believe he made losses; so he'd better look for his contribution to the big forthcoming occasion. She had already intimated friends, and big plans were already under way. He should not have done what he did without her consent; after all she helped in creating it for the Bonsala family. She did not take the risk for the Atani family; and 'they' must not know about this.

"Who are they?"

"I mean those who actually took the risk in creating the gateway for this wealth for us. In case your academic brain does not understand, those who burnt down the old lab to make way for the new one."

"So you know them…."

"Faith and works go hand in hand."

This set Biletu thinking and analysing the whole event; that is, what he could remember of what he was told. He became confused as to what conclusions to come to; nor was he sure how to handle them. Did she do it out of love for him and the family or out of greed? How could she, a supposedly God-fearing woman do this? She could not have thought far ahead because even at this early stage it was already bringing them problems.

Bintu, in her own analysis, concluded her husband was just peculiar, daft when it came to business matters, and not cut out to be rich. Somehow she still had a place in her heart for him. Or was she 'stuck' with him? She thought of the prayer requests of many of her friends. Some requested greater love and respect from their husbands; some would like theirs to stop illicit affairs and spend more time with the family; others requested prayers for less lavish party lifestyles and more attention to the children. She reflected in particular on Mrs. Obrom whose husband joined a cult group in order to become rich. She knew many who joined or even started Churches after committing atrocities. In the final analysis she, Mrs. Bintu Bonsala should thank her star. However her thoughts rested on her fortieth birthday party; she had to save face and not let her bragging go in vain. She promised herself it would be the last of such lavish celebrations; serious family life began at forty.

17. Vendetta

Dust over the sale of the chemicals business settled, preparations began in earnest for the party to which about two hundred guests were expected. The husband jokingly referred to it as 'the rave night'. He suggested her school assembly hall as the venue and her group band to supply the music; they played well at Gloria's christening.

"Not for big occasions like this," was the reply.

She settled for one of Chief Atani's function rooms. This would help break the boycott of the erstwhile big man. Biletu had to put in the small profit at the end of the sale, and also diverted what was intended for Charles towards the village house.

The occasion was indeed a flamboyant one; photographers included those from the media houses. There was good turn out from the university, college, and staff school. The venue was well decorated and the music was good.

The dance floor was packed full of gyrating men and women when suddenly there was power failure. The crowd knew better than to move. Everywhere was pitch dark except for a pin-hole light that was seen by a few moving with a couple of figures out of the hall through a side entrance. Light was soon restored and things were back to normal.

After a thoroughly enjoyable evening, people started making their way home. As expected, the weekend newspapers were full of reports and photographs of the party. While Bintu revelled in it, Biletu was indifferent to all the fuss.

The Tuesday papers carried various news items about Chief Atani. Some simply declared him missing, while some said he was dead. The Triumph report was more detailed. He was last seen publicly at a party held at one of his hotels. His wife who was with him when he died said that although his abductors did not wear masks, she did not know any of them nor would she be able to recognise them. She only heard them mumble something about the boy's blood. She swore she did not know what they were talking about.

When she was asked by the husband if she knew the perpetrators of such act, "How would I know?" was Bintu's reply. Various reasons were suggested as to why the wife was also kidnapped and then set free unharmed.

Fingers were pointed at a few people, one in particular; but there was no proof. Like many before his, Chief Atani's death went unaccounted for. The mogul was no longer alive, to dish out brown envelopes to probe his death. The family fortune had dwindled so much that J.J. could not afford the large amounts being demanded to investigate the case. In any case, he had to watch his back as well. His brother had long fled the country.

His fears were confirmed when, on a visit to his store one day, he found written on the metal door, "It's not your portion" in capital letters. What was the meaning of this? What was not his portion? To be killed? To die young? To be rich? He was truly perplexed.

At the Fellowship meeting the following day, he related it to the members, and asked for prayers to overcome any threat to his life. It was the anointed Mrs. Bonsala who saw a vision for him. There was an unclean spirit dwelling in that storehouse; and this was caused by the peculiar history behind the 'founding'. It was like Greek to J.J. Did she mean the foundation of the house, or the founding of the business or what? The vision continued; "It is the message from the Lord of Hosts that in order to rid yourself of any impediment to your business, you should give generously to the students' union on their forthcoming rag day. They will be raising funds for a new science block."

"Oh, as a member of the alumni association, I always give something."

"I don't mean the university students; I mean the college students' union."

The connection between the evil spirit in his store and the students' union was beyond his comprehension. But before he could ask for clarification, the woman full of the Holy Spirit went on, "You know some rogues go round collecting money for their own pockets; make sure you give the money to the right person."

"But how will I know the right person?"

"The Lord will give you the spirit of discernment. Believe and see. After that you can enjoy your wealth in peace." Still bewildered, J.J. thought, 'seek no evil, hear no evil.' Some members marvelled at the vision while others were envious of J.J. for such favour from God.

The next consignment of the reagents was arriving in ten days' time, and J.J. had to travel out to sign the papers and arrange for delivery. It was the same day as the rag day. As was the practice, the students were out early, meandering between cars, jingling their tins for money most of which was coins. A few approached J.J. and he also put some coins in the tins; but all the time he was wondering when and how the discernment would come. Just as he was losing hope, he saw three students approach his car. They took positions, one in front as if blocking his way; and one on each side. Instead of a tin, the one on his side opened out a large brown envelope and said "Give generously, sir. It's not your portion to ignore us." What more discernment could he want? Without hesitation he took out his own folded brown envelope and put it into the bigger one. Job done, the three disappeared, leaving J.J. to go his way. He felt he had seen one of them before, but could not remember where.

This time, the testimony was in private, to the person who foretold it. He related how it all happened, and thanked her. "May God continue to use you for His purpose."

"Amen. You can now go and enjoy your wealth in peace. You have given unto Caesar what is Caesar's." Bintu replied.

To confirm this, the message on his warehouse was now "The gift's your portion and your salvation; who shall you fear?" While these words in themselves were reassuring, J.J. was not at peace. The undercover agents must have shifted attention to him now that his father was dead. He was not really at peace; not with himself; not with the society he lived in.

****

The next time Biletu went home, he stopped to have another chat with his mother. She was glad he was now famous, and mixing with friends; he was now rich and driving a better car. She hoped that he would contribute to a befitting burial when she passed on. The mention of her passing on made him emotional and he felt closer to her than he had ever felt. He decided to have a straight talk with her; maybe if he put the blame squarely at her doorstep she would leave him alone. "Mother, I'm surprised you have changed so much, even though you have been back in the village a long time now. Have you forgotten how you and father brought us up to work hard and live honest lives? Well that's what I'm doing. Both of you always quoted Proverbs 22 verses 1 and 6 to us. Aren't you proud you've succeeded?"

"My son, those were the days when workers in the vineyard ate last, wore the poorest clothes, and walked the streets till corn grew on the soles of their feet instead of in the fields. Those days are gone. I know what goes on now. Charles tells me and I see some myself. The cooperative here is in trouble because the treasurer has sent his son abroad with other people's savings. Everyone is reaping where they did not sow."

"Is that why I should join?"

"Oh. I thought you joined already. I hear you are now doing well, appearing in the right circles, riding better car, enjoying life more."

"Yes Mother; I tried it for a while, but I did not like it. That type of life is not for me. How could I enjoy making the money when I knew it was not for me or my family to enjoy, it wasn't even for charity; it was for those who already

101

had. So I quit. After all there are enough of rich people to make the money go round; they don't need me."

"You mean it?"

"I mean it. In any case, the reason for my visit is to let you know that I'm planning early retirement. As soon as the house is completed, I will move the family here."

"You mean you will leave city life and your big job for the village? Does Bintu know? What about the children's education?"

As usual, he did not know which question to answer first. "Everything will be sorted out by that time."

18. Befitting Burials

Bintu's friend Caroline was just leaving when he arrived back home. "Oh you are arriving just in time. I was reluctant to leave your wife alone, but I have to see my mother as well." Without asking any questions, Biletu ran inside to see what the problem was. He found her sobbing and shaking violently. Both children were around her, so it must be something else.

Her father passed away suddenly on Friday afternoon; and being a Moslem, was buried within twenty-four hours. It was sad to see him buried without 'befitting' ceremony; moreover her husband was not around to give the emotional support she needed. He apologised profusely and comforted her as best as he could. Secretly he was sure the old man was given a send off befitting his religious rank and place in society. He could not help but muse at what 'befitting' meant in Fynecountry under such circumstances.

"The opportunity will come when we mark the anniversary of his death. I will have recovered from the expenses of my own party." Throughout the following days the Bonsalas received visitors and phone calls sympathising with them on the death of their beloved father. They attested to his good nature and uprightness; they would surely miss the old man. According to the culture, the bereaved had to provide snacks and drinks for the sympathisers. The Bonsalas were not amused.

Since the Federal Government took over the college, there had been rumours of a change in the headship; the provost must be a professor, and, as everyone in Fynecountry knew, a choice of the current minister for education. Biletu did not fulfil any of these. However, after the rocky start and periods of warnings and adjustments, his respect and popularity grew among both staff and students. The academic standard of the college was widely acclaimed. Therefore the rumours about change eventually fizzled away. Neither the job itself nor the academic community gave Biletu worries; it was the society at large that he wished he could escape from. His wife on the other hand could handle anything that came her way either for herself or her husband.

A few months after Bintu lost her father, news came of the sudden passing away of Mamabless--Biletu's mother. After spending part of the day with the harvest committee, she had her evening wash. She was about to have supper when she suddenly collapsed. All attempts to revive her failed. News of her passing soon spread far and near. While some people thanked God for such quiet and painless death, others mourned the end of freebies. She was a very generous woman who received very little for the orphanage she managed.

Biletu and Bintu could not believe what had hit them. There was no doubt that both of them were genuinely sad about the sudden loss of Mother; but one issue that kept cropping up was 'befitting burial'. How could they, in their financial state give a befitting burial Fynecountry-style to this woman for whom they had done relatively little in her lifetime and who deserved so much?

Bintu insisted on going to the village with the husband on his first trip for family meetings. She had to go and commiserate with the whole family; it was not proper to leave it till the burial ceremonies had started. Also she had to prepare the new house where they would stay.

Church members and village residents met regularly with the family to plan a befitting burial.

While the close family members were having discussions, Bintu sought Charles to thank him for overseeing the building of the house; not even a brother could do so much. Ever since he and her husband went to school together they had been close. May God bless him. She was sure there was nothing he would not do for his friend. Charles assured her it was a pleasure helping his friend and he was ready to continue to help.

Biletu brought unexpected news when he returned from the next family meeting. Charles came to interrupt the meeting. He apologised for doing so, knowing he was no blood relation of the family; but he was close enough to Mamabless to be considered her son. In fact the deceased considered him a son and entrusted her with many secrets, one of which he had come to divulge. He himself was not in favour of the contents, but he dreaded the repercussion of not obeying her; hence he had brought the last wishes of the woman to their notice. He took out a piece of paper which he handed to the eldest son.

It was a typed note supposed to be the last wishes of Mamabless. Her burial was to be a very simple one, howbeit a befitting Christian celebration of her life. She was to be buried wherever she breathed her last, and not be moved across villages. She had always hated the cold weather, so her body must not spend more than a couple of days in the mortuary; that is if necessary at all, just to give them time to make necessary arrangements. She was to be dressed in white, with no veil over her face; she wanted to see the way ahead so as not to end up in hell. "I came quietly, and I'm going quietly," read a sentence. (Everyone except Stella laughed). "And don't forget my eyebrow pencil; I won't look myself without it." She was aware of the fanfare in Fynecountry; there was to be no alcohol served by anybody throughout the ceremonies. There was to be no extravagance. There was a tomb beside her husband reserved for her. Any orphan left at the time of her death should be transferred to the state orphanage, and the staff paid off. The quarters used by the orphans could be converted into something for young children. Her family and close relations could disagree with this; hence she was dictating it to an 'adopted' and trusted son who was sure to see that her wishes were carried out. She would forever haunt anyone who went against these wishes. It was signed 'Mother a k a Mamabless'.

The contents of the note sparked off a big row among the group present. The note went from one hand to another, each person trying to figure out how genuine it was. No one seemed to have a document with Mother's handwriting and signature. However everyone was aware of her practice of dictating notes and signing the important ones. This one had her signature. Although a group leader in Church, she had not been writing lately; she had young men and women around her to whom she dictated notes. Hence the signature at the end was of great importance. Was it really Mother's? Biletu's sister was particularly furious. This was an opportunity for her to throw a lavish party. She was still young and just started work when her father died. She had always wanted a befitting burial for the mother.

Suddenly Bintu remembered a note Mother sent her through the husband, thanking her for the gift of a dress she sent. She was not sure she still had it; but she thought she might do, because Mother seldom wrote her so she treasured this particular one especially since it bore her signature. She promised to search for it.

The other issue of course was that of the scale of events. Everyone knew Mother had always wanted a befitting burial. "She even stressed this to me recently when I had a private chat with her," said Biletu.

"And to us as well," agreed the senior caretaker of the orphanage.

"The note is saying the same thing. I think the problem here is the definition of 'befitting' in each case," cut in Charles. "Mother wanted a Christian befitting burial; and she has helped by giving us the definition: nothing elaborate." They all looked at each other.

"How can such a stalwart be buried like a chicken? My mother is leaving this world with pomp and pageantry," protested the daughter.

"But she's already left," somebody joked.

"Yes but her body is yet to be escorted to the grave; and it's not going quietly," she insisted.

"Well, I would not want to go against the wishes of the deceased, because she was a respected member of the Church and community. Once we can prove that the signature is authentic, we have to abide by her wishes," Reverend Titus declared, and brought the meeting to a close with a prayer. There was no time to waste in case the last wishes were real. He urged Bintu to try and locate her own note for comparison; otherwise they would go ahead with the usual plan.

Back home, Biletu and Bintu discussed the note. He was sure it was false. How could Mother entrust such important document to Charles? Why not one of the children, or a Church leader? Surely some of the orphans she raised must have become lawyers. No one had ever heard her say 'Christian befitting'. According to the wife, this might be God's mysterious way of saving them from embarrassment. How would they have managed otherwise? Mother was the equivalent of a queen in the village and people would have come from far and near not only to eat and drink freely, but also to pass judgement on how 'befitting' the farewell was. She would search high and low for her own note; and she hoped the signatures would match. At least people would understand the reason for a quiet but decent burial. She could be buried quietly as her father was. That would give them time to save for bigger celebrations later.

Bintu could not attend the next meeting. She had taken too much time off; and after all she was a daughter-in-law, not a daughter. But sure enough she found the note and gave it to her husband who presented it to the meeting. Both signatures were held side by side, twisted, and turned by everyone present, each trying to spot the difference. In the end, both were declared the same. It was victory for a few, disappointment for many.

Preparations went into top gear. All Methodist Churches in the surrounding towns and villages were sent the programme of events; each child, each family member invited their own small groups. Despite the short notice a large crowd was still expected, especially as it was the dry season.

Local bands and masquerades that usually graced such occasions were of course banned from the Christian events. However, as Mother could not be escorted to Father without some rejoicing there had to be some singing and dancing. The village Methodist choir would not do a good job; so Bintu offered to bring her Church group. This sparked some disagreement between Bintu and Stella. Why should the daughter-in-law overshadow her at her mother's funeral? When asked if she could supply a suitable substitute at short notice, there was silence. Bintu's Church band performed brilliantly at the three-hour long wake and stayed overnight for the procession to the graveyard. Papa Cletus brought his private security company to help. Biletu was surprised that this man, who had become the Senior Security Officer managing the security staff of both the university and the college, still found it necessary to establish a private company. Everyone, Bintu included, seemed or wish to have at least two jobs.

Everyone was pleased with their effort, and satisfied that they had respected Mamabless's wishes. Biletu, when alone with his wife, actually thanked God for saving him the embarrassment of having to take a Bank loan. A divine intervention, as he put it. Bintu agreed with him She acknowledged the loyalty of friends; one in particular.

19. The People's Money

"There was a young guy whose face looked familiar, but who I could not remember. He was nicely dressed and drove a nice car too," said Biletu.

"You mean the one with the new Mercedes? That was Cletus. He's done very well for himself since graduation; he works for the diamond industry."

"I see; and his father is doing well too."

"Those are people who don't let opportunities pass them by. 'Grab it while you can' is their motto."

"What if you grab the wrong thing, or what's not yours?"

"You grab it and make it yours. You don't wait for it to fall into your laps."

"What of the chemical, I mean the reagents business; did I grab it, or did it fall into my laps? Maybe I did not grab it well, and it slipped away. Or maybe it was not meant for me. Don't you believe in destiny?"

"Not in all cases. In some cases I believe in connection, connection, connection."

Life returned to normal.

The local Methodist Diocese agreed to fund the education of the two orphans still resident when their benefactor died. Staff and neighbours were asked to take their belongings and vacate the premises for cleaning and refurbishment.

Biletu and his wife occasionally reminisced on all aspects of the ceremonies, and wondered if any more expenses or glamour would have made any difference to either her life on earth or her place beyond. The answer was a clear no. The only difference —and a big one at that—would have been in their pockets. They went on to discuss life in general in Fynecountry. It was then Biletu intimated his wife of his plan to take early retirement and live a quiet life. "And what are you going to do in the village, become a farmer?" asked Bintu angrily.

"And what's wrong in cassava or fish farming?" was the reply.

From then on Bintu took more interest in their property in the village, and seized the opportunity to see what was going on in the family house as well. Her brain worked so hard she often ended up with headaches.

Junior had just started secondary school and Gloria was in the nursery. The couple still managed conveniently on their income. However reality soon began to dawn on Biletu, as cost of living soared alongside school fees. Would they survive on his pension? What would Bintu do in the village? Bintu, on her part, knew exactly what she was going to do, although she kept it to herself. What worried her was what the husband would do in the village with a PhD in Chemistry. She made a prayer request at a Fellowship meeting; for the Lord to guide him and provide a way.

News soon reached the college community and the student union that their provost was planning early retirement, but would have nothing to go to. Somewhere along the line rumours of federal government harassment were added; some highly-placed individual wanted to replace him with their own person. While some thought it was foolish of him to leave with nowhere to go to, others sympathised with his plight with the federal government. Not even Bintu could understand, let alone explain how anyone would take such drastic steps to escape from a society in which he had lived for so long, and at the expense of his family. On Biletu's part he could not see himself surviving in it for much longer without getting into difficulties; not with his job, but with friends and a wife whose outlook was different. Bintu on the other hand did not see how they could survive for much longer; end of story.

Biletu was on his way to a lecture hall when a smartly-dressed guy stepped out of an elegant Mercedes. He recognised him as the same man who greeted him warmly at his mother's funeral; Cletus. "Excuse me sir," he said, indicating that he wished to talk to him. After all Biletu was his former provost and much older. The diligent provost/lecturer replied that he had come at a wrong time as he was on his way to a lecture. Could he come at another time? An appointment with his secretary would be a good idea. This reception did not surprise Cletus, who then went in to book an appointment.

Biletu later told his wife of the brief encounter. "Does he think I'm interested in diamonds? I have better things to do with my money."

"What if he has come to throw some into your laps, won't you grab them?"

"And do what with them? It's like throwing pearls to pigs. Although I'm not a pig; I'm a decent, contented, law-abiding citizen."

"Yes; and one who will end up living like a pig. Now, seriously if his visit is anything to do with diamonds, buying, selling, or even stealing them, send him my way."

"I don't think it's to do with diamonds anyway; people know me better than to approach me with such rubbish. He may want a job as a graduate assistant; that's all he's qualified for. He'll have to do a lot more for anything higher."

"And end up with letters behind his name and no cash to back it up? Don't worry; the guy is too comfortable to want to white-wash his designer suits with chalk."

The secretary announced the presence of a Mr. James. Biletu knew it was Cletus. He expected him to have come with either an application letter, or a specimen---of diamond. Instead, he made himself comfortable, asked after his family, and told him a bit about himself. While he was doing this, Biletu switched on the tape recorder under his desk. He was still a bachelor, but had a steady girlfriend. He was in business, a lucrative one and one that gave no hassle whatsoever. Biletu thought "Even armed robbery comes with some hassle, if it is to succeed."

Cletus continued "I'm into lifting."

'Lifting' was the local term for illegal but well established acquisition and onward sale of diamond in Fynecountry. He likened it to oil bunkering in some oil-producing countries. Only the privileged few had access to it. Everyone knew about it, but there was nothing anyone could do other than to aspire to also be a beneficiary. The purpose of his visit was to offer him a 'hand of friendship'. "Sir, it's your portion to accept this offer and retire a rich man able to look after his family for the rest of his life. This is an opportunity being thrown into your laps."

"This expression sounds familiar," thought Biletu. "Sounds good to me; in fact too good to be true. I'm afraid I need time to think about it, and even seek advice."

"Fine, sir. The supply won't dry up or disappear; but, sir, it's not something you shout about. Keep it within the family."

"Before you go, can I ask why you are doing this for me? Where is the catch, and when am I to expect the police?"

"My mother has great respect for you. She said you saved her from either an early death or an early divorce from my father."

"I don't understand."

"Apparently you saved her from good beating from my father when he was locked out in the rain. Now she's enjoying life to the full."

"Another mysterious work of God!" exclaimed Bintu after listening to the husband. But she did not trust the husband with such rare opportunity. "Why don't you let me handle this?" she pleaded.

"No. It fell into my laps, not yours."

"But you won't grab it; even if you do, you may not grip tight and it will slip off---forever."

"Believe me, I will grip tight; so tight the precious metal will talk."

"Precious metal shines, glitters, it doesn't talk."

"Well in my hands it will do both."

"Just do what is best for us."

Biletu could not believe his luck. Never in a million years would he have imagined such easy way to make money; good money. He kept to the advice not to shout about it; it was quiet, cool cash flowing in.

The Retirement

Despite the material wealth Biletu was still averse to life around him; and the fear that his wife would want to stay on plagued him. But to his amazement she joined in plans towards his retirement to the village. He got the first inkling of the reason when one day she reintroduced the issue of her starting a nursery school and being her own boss.

"How is that possible with our move to the village? Are you planning a divorce?"

"No way. In fact I plan to help fulfil one of Mother's last wishes."

"If I know you well, you are planning your own version of befitting burial now that we have some money. Please let Mother rest in peace."

"She's going to look down on us and bless us; but that's if the family allows me to use the orphans' premises for my nursery school. Remember her request for children to be around all the time?"

"You crafty woman; no wonder your protest to our move to the village died down. But who in the village is going to patronize your type of nursery school, which I'm sure won't be cheap?"

"I've been thinking; and planning. My visits to the house were not without a reason."

Bintu was sure her plans would work if only Stella, who had now become an enemy, would not stand in the way. She decided on a direct approach; she was prepared to appeal to, even beg her. The older brother would see the move as an asset. Or would he? He was now the head of the family, having the final say. Moreover, he had lived in the village for much longer, commanded respect, and probably had plans of his own for the premises. So she should not take things for granted. Her foresight did not fail her.

Big Brother had always sought to expand his piggery and add a poultry and if possible a fish pond. There was great demand for the products in the cities and various establishments. Money was his problem. Allowing the younger Bonsalas to go ahead with their plan would be an exchange for his own dreams to come true.

There was no mincing of words when the whole plan was presented to Big Brother. It was a win-win situation. It did not matter whether it was a daughter or daughter-in-law keeping the family name alive. Mamabless Nursery School was a good idea. Stella gave in since she could not come up with better ideas. She concentrated on her travelling career, and everyone else had something to occupy their time. Bintu was allowed to make reasonable alterations to the premises now referred to as 'the nursery'.

Mamabless Nursery School was to be a high-brow residential school which catered for the young children of busy career-oriented professionals in the cities. The parents had the choice of long- stay or weekly boarding. The package included living and educational expenses. With Bintu's educational, religious and social background, she was sure applications for such facility would pour in. Also with her connection, connection, connection philosophy she had no problem in getting government provisional approval. Within a short period of their move to the village, jobs would be created for many, Charles in the forefront; and the whole village would begin to take on a new look.

Biletu's send-off ceremony was attended by celebrities from all over the state; there were representatives from the Federal Ministry of Education as well, everyone bearing witness to his uprightness. Bintu was recognised as the strong woman who had been ahead of the sceptical man to prepare his way, behind him to urge him on, and beside him to support him. How true.

At last, Dr and Mrs Biletu Bonsala and family were set to live a quiet, contented life in and from the village, having tasted both sides of life in Fynecountry and paved the way for what they hoped would suit them better.

Neighbours expected big removal vans to come to do the transfer to the Bonsala's new location; but they were disappointed, because the couple had decided to take few of the old stuff with them. It was going to be new house, new furniture, new way of life. However, this lack of removal fanfare sparked off various rumours. The family must be relocating abroad; the former provost had been offered a professorial job in one of the universities in London. They reckoned the reason why Junior had been registered in the Ismei High School for Boys was for him to learn discipline and academic excellence at home; English school children talked back at teachers, some even swore at them. He might even suffer discrimination and be prevented from achieving his potential. Good schools were cheaper at home.

Bintu had furnished the village two-storey residence with expensive items. Each of the four rooms had nice fitted furniture; so did the lounge and kitchen. The upper front door opened on to a good size balcony, below which grew some hibiscus and bougainvillea trees. The fence around the property had to be reshaped and extended to enclose the old orphanage. This was an extensive adjustment, but money was no problem; the young children had to be safe. Among the essentials in the back garden was a well; water supply in the villages was erratic.

As they were settling down into their new environment, Bintu was at the same time ordering equipment and furniture for her residential nursery/primary school. It was at this stage that the enormity of her plans started to dawn on her. Even she could not understand how her normally-sharp foresight failed her. Although she was convinced she was providing a much-needed service, and was able to tick many of the boxes concerning the infrastructure, clientele, and facilities, some issues beyond her control now stared her in the face. Her type of clientele would only fuel the appetite of the highway robbers known to frequent the area. How many would be prepared to take the risk? But life had to go on; it could not be on hold for the sake of evil people. 'He that is in me is greater than the devil in those robbers.' Her excitement grew each day as she watched the delivery of new beds and mattresses, tables, chairs, crockery and other items to the premises.

The momentum was however interrupted by the reminder that it was only two weeks to the anniversary of her father's death. It was no welcome news to Bintu at that particular time; not because she had no money (there was plenty of that), but her enthusiasm was not in top gear since something else had priority. However since she did not disappoint her friends when she had little money, she was not going to do so now that she had been blessed. She switched attention for the next few days, making necessary preparations to prove that although she now lived in the village, she was still a city woman. She had also planned that she would take the opportunity to remind them of her ambition and solicit patronage.

To her greatest disappointment, only a handful of them turned up; reason: it was Caroline's fortieth birthday in Olito. Bintu took this as a reminder that she was no longer one of them; her time was over and someone else had taken her place. "There is a season for everything," the Bible says. Fortunately for her, it was a strictly-Moslem affair, so the absence of her fellowship group and Church band was not too noticeable. Nevertheless she could not help admitting to herself that this time the scales fell from her eyes; not the husband's. Maybe she should take a leaf from Paul's conversion in Acts 9 verse 18 and the transformation of his life that followed.

****

On their return to Aribou, she resumed her plans for the village-with-a-difference; too busy to miss former friends. Biletu on his part was still adjusting to village life and waking up every morning with nowhere to go, no notes to prepare, no chemicals to mix. Whenever he bemoaned his situation, his wife reminded him that that was the meaning of early retirement; early retirement to the village at that!

Schools were on holidays, so he decided to take walks and drive round the schools and chat with whoever was around. He made it a fact-finding mission for himself, making a critical assessment of everything he came across.

During one of his travels he stopped to have a chat with Charles who suggested he visit the Bible school in the next village; he could register for a course in theology and have something to occupy the rest of his days.

"Bible school! As a student or as a teacher? To preach or to practise?" was the reaction.

"Well, you want something to do with your time. Or you can come and work with us in the animal farm. It's enjoyable and it's worthwhile. Your brother is looking for someone to improve the animal feed. Come and lend a helping hand."

"Aribou is a fertile place; he just needs to tap the resources."

"Maybe he will know what you are talking about; I don't."

Each went his own way.

When he got home, Bintu eagerly showed him all the items she had bought from the nearby town for Junior, in preparation for his boarding school. His lack of interest was noticeable; but that was her husband, strange man.

The following morning, Bintu was supervising the staff she had employed in arranging the furniture in what was to be the dormitory. When she turned around she was pleased to see the husband behind her.

"As if you read my mind; I was just going to seek your advice on how to arrange the lockers, beside the beds or at the foot; and behold you appeared."

"Yes. Actually, I've come to see where Gloria's bed is going to be."

"Gloria's bed! What are you talking about? Gloria is not a..a..a, I mean she's....."

"You are right. She's not an orphan. Neither are any of the children you are taking away from their parents at tender ages!"

"You kill-joy! How can you say this? I thought the devil in you had disappeared; I can see he's still lurking somewhere."

"The devil is not stopping you; he's only saying that if this place is good enough for the children of professionals like you, it should be alright for yours as well. In fact Gloria has an advantage over the others. Her parents are nearby."

Bintu could not believe what she was hearing. After all she had done and prepared to make the place comfortable and safe for the young children, providing a much-needed service. She still did not understand her husband's problem, nor could she bring herself to agree with him.

"Leaving home at an early age could be an advantage to the children of busy professionals. They learn early to mix, and their parents are free to pursue their careers and be productive in society, without child care worries. The children get good night sleep, and hence good health. Sound mind in sound body, home away from home; that's my aim."

"I'm only asking that Gloria enjoy some of the privilege."

"So when, in your view, is it right for a child to leave home? Why is Junior going to Ismei High School then?"

"I was coming to that. Junior is old enough to go to boarding secondary school. And in any case, I've decided he's staying right here and going to the village school."

Bintu slumped on to the bed behind her while one of the women ran for a glass of water. The husband just looked on. She would soon get over the shock; which she soon did; indeed. She then burst into tears, lamenting how her child, a privileged child, the son of an ex-provost, would go to a rural school. Biletu went on to name several friends who went to village secondary schools and had risen to responsible posts in Fynecountry. It was the academic standard and discipline in the school that mattered, not the location.

"But I've heard that this school here is now rubbish."

"That will soon change, when I join the staff. Yes I'm going to offer my services for free. I'm going to equip their laboratories; the school will soon become one of JJ's clients. Charles said Big Brother would like better grade of feed for his animals. It will be produced right here in the village. I'm going to work with the students to develop and produce it in the school laboratory. Other animal farmers will benefit as well and supplies will yield income to the school. It is the money of the people returning to the people."

"You are only being selfish; pursuing your own interests while destroying mine. After all I've done for you. You know I have always wanted to run my own school in the city. But because of your wish to retire early, I had to modify my plans. What do you expect me to do with the furniture that has been delivered? How will I fulfil Mother's last wishes?"

"Your idea looks good on paper; hence it was approved. But how many of those big city workers will risk their lives and those of their children to travel the rugged and unsafe roads to come here? What staff have you got? Moreover, you don't need their money. Cletus has already made us custodians of the people's money, and we have to give it back to them; somehow."

"Is that what he told you when he extended the hand of friendship?"

"No, but what do you expect me to do with the large sums coming in for which I have not worked?"

"You've been receiving stolen goods then."

"Yes, to return them to the rightful owners; another one of God's mysterious ways."

"I'm surprised you are receiving them at all, instead of exposing the thieves; if I know you well."

"You should know when not to expose thieves."

"When?"

"When by so doing you will be exposing yourself and your loved ones to danger."

Words failed Bintu. He was right. In Fynecountry, that would be treading on dangerous grounds.

"I can see you are at a loss as to what to do. Donate the items to the state orphanage; I will refund the money to you. You belong with the masses, Bintu; not with the system. I see Romans 12 verse 2 is highlighted in your Bible. 'Be ye not be conformed to this world; but be transformed by the renewing of your mind, that you may prove what is that good and acceptable and perfect will of God'. There's no one you want to conform to in the village; so be transformed." (The idea of transformation again!)

"And what about all the alterations I've made to the house, ready for Mamabless School; nursery or whatever?"

"As long as money is not an issue, I don't think it matters what you do for children; so think of alternatives to honour Mother's memory. When Jesus invited children to Himself, He didn't ask them to come and live with Him. Mother wanted children around, not necessarily to live here." Bintu was quite impressed with the husband's quotations from the Bible. Village life has given him time to read the word of God. Are they swapping roles now?

His advice set Bintu thinking. Why should she continue to limit herself to the idea of a nursery school, since they no longer lived in the city and money was no longer a problem for them? The idea of adult literacy school crossed her mind; but the mention of children in 'the last wishes' note kept bugging her. What had she led herself into? It looked like she was the author of her own dilemma. She decided to seek the help of the only other person with whom she shared the secret of the true origin of the note; Charles.

****

Since Charles's employment as supervisor in the animal farm, he had most weekends free and had become a lay preacher in the Church. He popped round to invite his old friend and his family to Church the following day, as he was preaching the sermon. He urged Biletu to try and join his brother in continuing the family influence in the Church. Bintu took the opportunity to have a private word with him.

His cleverness in helping to create the idea of Mamabless nursery school was amazing. Could he please also help out in the present circumstances?

"I'll think of something. God will make a way. See you in Church tomorrow."

The sermon was based on the Old Testament reading; Exodus chapter 2. The preacher expounded on how a baby destined to be killed at birth through a human decree was saved by divine intervention. God used different calibres of women – from his poor mother, through his sister and palace maidens to the princess – to save Moses so he could fulfil God's purpose in his life. But for these women, Moses would have died of starvation or been swept away by the river. His mother's effort in minimising the risk of drowning, and the sister's wisdom to watch in hiding were both commended. The morale of this, according to the preacher, was for women to rise up to their role in society. Perinatal mortality and infant deaths in surrounding villages were high; and many could be prevented. The traditional birth attendants needed better training and equipment to function properly. This could not be achieved without money, expertise and infrastructure. The Red Cross was looking for a place to run child health clinics twice a week; there was none in Aribou village. Women should get together and find a solution.

"Thus says the Lord of Hosts. God bless you all."

Both Biletu and Bintu admired their friend. Despite his limited education he was able to convey his message and impress the congregation in a mixture of English and the local language.

It was the second time God was speaking to him directly in that Church, Biletu acknowledged. The first time He advised on how to let mammon serve him; this time it was how to let mammon serve the village. Not bad. No pontificating; just straightforward practical talk. He congratulated his friend.

The spirit of discernment did not fail Bintu who finally and reluctantly decided to abandon the idea of money-making nursery in favour of a maternity and child health clinic run by the Red Cross and largely funded by the extended hand of friendship from Biletu. She could still justify her use of the converted orphanage to the Bonsala family. After all Big Brother was in the congregation as well when the idea was suggested.

Biletu joined the staff of the secondary school; first as deputy head and soon after he became the headmaster. This time, Junior did not resent being called the headmaster's son.

The highlight of the second anniversary of Mother's death was the opening of Mamabless Child Health Centre. Among the guests were Biletu's former staff and students from Olito, including Cletus. After warm handshakes and a tour of the premises, Cletus gave his former provost thumbs up. No better person could have been entrusted with the people's money.

Aribou prospered fast, attracting back to the village many of its sons and daughters who had abandoned their birth place to struggle in the big cities. An oasis was thereby created in which the inhabitants lived by a different code of conduct. Crazymoney acquired a new and respected dimension. The name Bonsala eventually became indelibly written in the history of Aribou in Fynecountry.

One morning, as Biletu got ready for work, he heard humming coming from the bathroom, and remembered the words to the tune. They were:

Dear Lord and Father of mankind

Forgive our foolish ways

Re-clothe us in our rightful mind

In purer lives thy service find

In deeper reverence praise

Author Biography

Eppie Goyea attended Queen's College, Lagos, Nigeria and later the United Missionary College, Ibadan before leaving for further studies abroad.

On her return, she worked briefly as a health educator with the Lutheran World Federation during the post-war period in the then Rivers State. She later joined the staff of the Institute of Child Health, University of Benin where she worked until her relocation to the UK in the late 1980's.

As an avid reader of fiction and true life stories, she has always hoped to write one herself. She has published an information booklet and several articles in reputable journals related to preventive child health.

In A Tale From Fynecountry, Eppie illustrates some aspects of life in developing countries through fictitious characters.

She is now retired and lives in Stevenage, Hertfordshire.